MURDER AT THE CIRCUS

A GINGER GOLD MYSTERY BOOK 19

LEE STRAUSS

la
plume
PRESS

Library and Archives Canada Cataloguing in Publication

Title: Murder at the Circus / Lee Strauss,

Names: Strauss, Lee (Novelist), author.

Series: Strauss, Lee (Novelist). Ginger Gold mystery ; 19.

Description: Series statement: A Ginger Gold mystery ; 19 | "A 1920s cozy historical mystery."

Identifiers: Canadiana (print) 20220142939 | Canadiana (ebook) 20220142947 | ISBN 9781774092101 (hardcover) | ISBN 9781774092088 (softcover) | ISBN 9781774092095 (IngramSpark softcover) | ISBN 9781774092118 (Kindle) | ISBN 9781774092125 (EPUB)Classification: LCC PS8637.T739 M8725 2022 | DDC C813/.6—dc23

GINGER GOLD MYSTERIES

(IN ORDER)

Murder at the Royal Albert Hall

Murder in Belgravia

Murder on Mallowan Court

Murder at the Savoy

Murder at the Circus

Murder at the Boxing Match

Murder in France

"*Y*our son is missing."

Had she heard the headmaster of Kingswell Academy correctly? Mrs. Ginger Reed, known by some as Lady Gold, stared at the black receiver of her rotary desk phone and then spoke into it. "I beg your pardon, Mr. Boyle?"

"Your son Samuel is missing."

Ginger blinked at Scout's formal name. "What do you mean, missing? Did he miss a lesson? Perhaps he's late back from a walk? You know how lads lose track of time."

The headmaster released a sigh. "No, madam. His bed wasn't slept in. His things are gone. He must've packed a knapsack after the evening inspection and sneaked away after dark. I'm terribly sorry.

We do everything we can to rein in our most troubled—"

"Most troubled?"

"Yes, well, you are aware that young Master Reed has had difficulty adjusting."

Ginger and her husband Basil, a chief inspector at Scotland Yard, had decided to send Scout to boarding school in January. They probably should've sent him the autumn before, but they'd only adopted the lad two years earlier. After spending his child-hood on the streets of London, barely cared for by an ailing uncle, it seemed rather too much to expect him to jump into a uniform and blend in with the chil-dren of the elite when he'd barely just stopped drop-ping his *Hs*.

It was only after Scout's uncle had died and his older cousin Marvin Elliot had joined the Royal Navy—an alternative to the prison he was headed to had Ginger not intervened—that Scout became Ginger's ward. Then, once she and Basil had married, they adopted Scout.

All had gone swimmingly until the birth of Rosa, after which Scout felt he'd lost his position of favour with his parents.

The timing of sending Scout to boarding school was unfortunate, but purely coincidental. In no uncertain terms, she and Basil hadn't sent their son away to remove him from their family—of course not! They sent him for the same reason all parents sent their children to school—to give them the best education and opportunity in life.

Sadly, Scout hadn't seen it that way despite Ginger and Basil's reassurances.

"Have you asked his friends?" Ginger asked. "Surely, someone must know where he is."

Another imperceptible sigh. "Master Reed has had, er, difficulties making friends, madam. He refused to engage in activities and do anything to integrate himself with his peers."

Ginger's chest squeezed with worry and regret. They should've taken their son's unhappiness more seriously.

"I see," she said. "Have the police been notified?"

"Yes, madam."

"Please do keep me informed. My husband and I shall do what we can to find him on our end. Hopefully, he's finding his way home."

In her study, Ginger sunk into the chair at the large desk that had once belonged to her father. She stared blankly at his portrait, painted when he was younger than she was now. Scout knew how to take care of himself on the streets. If any child—at thirteen, he could hardly be called a child much longer—could make his way on his own, it would be him.

His safety was of concern to Ginger, but her heart broke that her son had felt unloved and unwanted, so much so that he'd taken this drastic step.

Yes, he had the ability to survive, but that didn't make his situation less dangerous; in fact, if his cousin Marvin were any indication, it would most certainly lead him to a life of crime.

As if sensing Ginger's distress, Boss, Ginger's Boston terrier, roused himself from his bed by the fireplace and went to her side. She patted his little black-and-white head as he laid his chin on her knee.

"Oh, Bossy. What has our boy done?"

Ginger was about to lift the receiver when it rang. Basil's voice came through, loud and clear.

"Ginger?"

Ginger pictured Basil's worried face, the deepening lines around attractive hazel eyes, greying temples growing greyer with this new concern. "I just spoke to Mr. Boyle," she returned.

"Scout's run away," Basil said. "I've heard from the local police."

"What do we do?"

"There's not much to do, love. Our men are on the lookout now."

"Very well." Ginger pushed a wayward lock of her red, bobbed hair behind her ear. It wasn't that she didn't have confidence in the London Metropolitan Police, it was that she had more confidence in Scout's ability to evade them.

Ginger rarely felt as she did now, unsure of what to do next. She left the study, searching for Pippins, her darling butler, with Boss following behind, his nails clicking on the tiled floor.

"Pips," she called out when she caught sight of the back of the butler's balding head. "Has the mid-morning post arrived?"

"It's just arrived, madam," Pippins said, turning to her voice.

Tall and slender with bowing shoulders and skin wrinkled in map-like lines, Ginger's long-time and long-suffering septuagenarian butler presented a silver tray with a single piece of post on it.

"No envelope, madam," Pippins said. "Just a folded piece of paper slipped through the letterbox."

"How odd," Ginger said, plucking the paper off the tray. A quick peruse to identify the author caused her heart to flutter.

"It's from Marvin Elliot."

"Yes, madam. I didn't read the contents, but I couldn't help seeing the sender's name."

Ginger felt her cheeks redden as she quickly read the poorly scribbled notation riddled with bad grammar and spelling errors.

Dear Lady Gold,

Scout is wiv me and safe enuf. They kicked me out of the navy cos of fightin too much and that I punched an officer by mistake.

I'll take kair of Scout for now but I rekon you mite want to come and get im at the circus in Clapham.

"IS EVERYTHING ALL RIGHT, MADAM?"

"I'm afraid not, Pippins. Scout's cousin has left the navy and joined the circus."

"How unfortunate," Pippins said.

"And Scout's gone with him. Oh mercy. Pips, please tell Clement to ready my motorcar."

2

*Y*oung Scout Elliot Reed stood on a knoll overlooking Clapham Common and unshouldered his heavy leather knapsack. Though mid-May, the late morning air was crisp. Rather than making him feel chilly, Scout felt invigorated. He'd seen loads in his thirteen years of life, more than many fellows his age, but he had seen nothing like this. He put his bag on the ground and gazed in wonderment at the scene below him.

On the grassy field, and just visible above the sprawling common trees, were dozens of brightly coloured canvas tents circling a massive one with distinctive blue and white stripes.

"The big top," he said aloud, his breath forming an instant mist in the cool air. The whole formation was surrounded by high, collapsible wooden fencing. The main tent was easily twenty times larger than the smaller tents, some of which weren't yet fully erected, and the wooden structures surrounding it. Scout's eyes grew even bigger when he suddenly realised elephants were pulling on the ropes to erect the main tent poles. Elephants! Men were directing the enormous animals with small sticks as they shouted instructions barely audible from where Scout stood.

"Blimey!"

A newspaper advertisement he'd recently seen had filled his imagination for three days. The scene before him now filled up his whole horizon as well. His heart quickened as he considered what he was about to do.

Being of small stature, Scout always had to work just a bit harder and perhaps be just a bit braver than other lads he'd known on the streets of London. He was no stranger to being on his own, and this experience had given him the pluck to escape Kingswell Academy, located to the west in Wandsworth, and the iron-fisted headmaster, Mr. Boyle.

During the night, he'd made his way on foot to Clapham. It'd been a long, cold walk, but he had dressed for it. He'd even brought some cheese and biscuits that he'd nicked from the main kitchen larder, valuable items for any escapee. He hadn't done anything like that for a long time, but he was glad to know that his survival instincts were still intact.

Throwing his knapsack onto his back, Scout took one look behind him, mostly out of habit, and then started down the knoll. His eyes focused on the huge sign over the main wooden gate that read "Sweeney's Spectacular Circus".

Scout made his way through the streets surrounding Clapham Common until he got within sight of the fence. A big, gruff-looking man stood by the main gate. Scout dodged out of view behind the many circus workers before the guard noticed him. A few minutes later, he found a section of the fence not yet properly fastened to the adjoining panels. It only took a moment to force the thing inwards enough to let him drop his knapsack inside and then another moment for him to squeeze his slight frame between the posts.

Finding himself at the rear of one of the smaller tents, Scout circled to the left. He was counting on no one looking at him twice amongst the many workers, some of whom were close to his age, and everyone focused on getting the place ready for the advertised opening night. Everywhere Scout looked men pulled on tent ropes, hammered up signs, and shouted instructions. Women swept the entryways and helped to erect food stands. The pungent smell of animal dung and sawdust filled the air.

"Scout?"

Scout spun at the incredulous yet familiar voice.

"That's not you, is it?"

Scout's lips pulled into a toothy smile. "Marvin!" He slapped his thigh. "How lucky am I to have found you so quickly!"

Marvin Elliot, Scout's older cousin, didn't share in Scout's elation. A frown deepened on a face that had grown wider and older. Marvin was slim rather than skinny, and Scout couldn't miss that his cousin's muscles had become more pronounced. Scout hoped his own stick-like appendages would soon develop similarly. Sitting behind a desk at some stuffy school wouldn't make that happen. Good, demanding work at the circus was the ticket to becoming a man like Marvin.

"It is you!" Marvin said, his eyes narrowing into slits. "What the devil, Scout?"

"Hey, Marvin. I saw an advert in one of the newspapers for circus workers, and I remembered your letter."

"So yer volunteered to be part of the set-up crew?" Marvin said, softening slightly. "But 'ow did yer get permission from the 'eadmaster? And Lady Gold?" He cocked his head to the side. "You skived off, dintcha?"

Scout shrugged.

"An', yer didn't volunteer, neither."

"No."

Looking stern, Marvin parked his hands on his hips and stared down at Scout. For a moment, Scout feared his cousin would shoo him away, but then Marvin's lips pulled into a crooked smirk.

"Come on then," Marvin said. After a glance around the grounds, he motioned towards a small alleyway between a tent and a wooden trailer. When they got to the rear of the trailer, Marvin opened a latch on a small wooden door. Inside were two camp beds, a wood-burning stove, a table with two chairs, and a chest of drawers. The wooden floor was clean and swept, and there were windows on either side. Both had cloth curtains now drawn closed.

There was enough space to move around, and the ceiling was just high enough for Marvin to stand up straight. A low-burning fire burned in the stove, making the place feel warm and welcoming; a faint curry scent tickled Scout's nose. He appreciatively whistled as he looked around the place.

"I share this with the elephant trainer, Mr. Singh," Marvin said as he gestured for Scout to have a seat at the table. "It's all right, I suppose, but it ain't nuthin' like the lap o' luxury you've been in for the last few years."

Scout bristled but couldn't think fast enough to respond.

"You 'ungry?" Marvin asked.

"No," Scout said. "I brought a bit of food from the school. I wouldn't mind a spot of tea, though, if you're offering."

"*A spot of tea?*" Marvin burst out laughing as he moved towards the stove. "You sound like the Duke of Fife or somefin'."

Scout protested, his cheeks suddenly feeling hot. "I do not!"

"*I do not,*" Marvin said, mimicking the elite. "You've turned into a nob, talkin' all posh like. You was already soundin' different last time I saw yer, but now yer really sound sophistica'ed." Marvin chuckled again as he put a tin of old tea onto the stove to warm it. "Well, I s'pose that's all right. It don't 'urt that someone from the Elliot family can speak proper like."

Scout's eyebrows came together. Marvin's observation unnerved him.

"I'm same as you, Marvin," he returned, summoning his former speech pattern. "Nuffin's changed."

Marvin's expression turned serious. "Yer knew when yer escaped from boardin' school there'd be trouble, maybe even people lookin' for yer. But yer came anyway. I'm glad t' see you o'course but . . ." He waved his hand. "C'mon then, out wiv it. Why are yer 'ere?"

"Boarding school ain't for me, that's all," Scout said dismissively.

Marvin let out a long sigh. "I s'pose that's the Elliot blood in yer. I didn't take much to bein' in the navy meself. All them officers yellin' orders at yer. More rules and regulations than a man can stand. Eh —" He wagged a finger in Scout's face. "I broke some rules and got in trouble, but I learned a fing or two." His large hands formed into fists, and he put them up in front of himself like a boxer. "I learned 'owta use these. I can't say it was all bad."

Marvin wrapped a rag around his hand and picked up the hot tin of warmed-up tea. He carefully poured it into a mug for Scout, adding thick condensed milk from a sticky-looking tin. Scout winced at the tepid and foul taste but drank it anyway.

"So then, after I show you around 'ere a bit, and yer get yer fill of the circus for a day or two, are yer goin' back to your family?" Marvin asked. "After you teach 'e, a lesson, or whatever it is yer fink you're doin'?"

"No, they don't want me." The force of the emotion that rose in Scout surprised him.

Marvin scoffed. "Don't be daft. Of course they want yer. I seen the way Lady Gold and her mister treat you. Like you was their very own son! Somefin' like that only 'appens in dreams and fairy tales, Scout. I dunno what you done to deserve it, but you've really struck it rich." Marvin shrugged his shoulders, leaned back, and shook his head. "Eh? I'm right, ain't I?"

Scout scowled, pushing his bad-tasting tea away.

"Don't tell me yer cocked it up some'ow!" Marvin leaned forward again. "You 'ad everyfin' there. A good place to sleep, proper schoolin', a family what loves yer, a promisin' future . . . you 'ad it made, Scout!"

"I didn't cock it up!" Scout shouted. "It was the baby."

Bewildered, Marvin sputtered, "W-what? What baby?"

"Mum, er, I mean, Mrs. Reed had a baby. Dintcha know?"

Marvin shook his head. "I don't read the society rags."

"Rosa, they named 'er."

"You mean like the SS *Rosa*?" Marvin raised his eyebrows. "That's a nice name."

"Yeah, cute as a button, she is," Scout said. "I got nuffin' against an 'elpless babe, but 'ow can I compete with that?"

"It's not a bleedin' competition," Marvin said. He gave Scout a friendly punch in the arm. "Look, you're still new to 'avin an actual family, so I guess yer wouldn't know 'ow these fings work. But I 'ave to tell yer that parents, good ones like the ones you 'ave, they 'ave enough love for both of yer. Love don't get smaller but multiplies with each new little tot."

"Bollocks," Scout returned. "That's not what I got. They spent all their time all fussin' and carin' for—"

"It's a babe! In need of a load of fussin' and carin'. It's only natural."

"'Ow would you know?"

Marvin waved his hand dismissively.

"Forget it," Scout said. "I ain't come to argue wiv yer. Can you get me on? I 'ave experience tendin' animals, after all. That's what I did on the SS. *Rosa*. An' I know 'ow to get along with people, 'specially those that ain't rich."

Scout's mind went to Boss, Lady Gold's Boston terrier he'd cared for on the SS *Rosa*. He and the dog had been good pals when Scout lived at Hartigan House, but—his stomach soured again—Boss was just another thing he'd lost when his "parents" had exiled him to boarding school.

Marvin cleared the table. "I'll be sacked if I get caught skiving. Since your 'eels are in, I'll take yer under my wing." He scrubbed Scout's wheat-grass hair, messing it even more than it was already. "'Ope you're prepared to work 'ard, me old china. This ain't a holiday."

"I'm ready," Scout said determinedly. "Let's go."

3

"*H*e's joined the circus!"

Ginger gripped the telephone receiver tightly as she relayed the news to Basil. "Marvin sent a note, scribbled on the back of a scrap of paper, saying Scout arrived earlier this morning. I'm about to leave to get him."

"Now, hold on, love," Basil said. "Clapham's the other side of the river. I'm coming to you now."

"But—"

"Nothing's going to happen to him between now and then. We know where he is and who he's with. He's safe."

Ginger blew a raspberry of frustration. Basil was right, of course. She couldn't very well traipse through the circus, grab Scout by the ear, and drag him home—though that was exactly what she wanted to do!

"Please do hurry," she said. "The sooner we bring him home, the better."

Ginger found she'd been on edge since their run-in with the sadistic Miss Vera Sharp two months earlier. The woman held Basil responsible for putting her father in prison and had a personal vendetta against him. Unfortunately, she'd had the wiles to escape the clutches of the police, and Ginger wouldn't rest until she was apprehended.

She returned the receiver to its cradle and then stared at Boss, who, on his haunches, stared back with round brown eyes. "What do we do about our Scout, hey boy?"

Boss, his stubby tail switching back and forth, nudged her with his wet nose as if to offer comfort. Ginger swooped him into her arms and pressed her chin to his soft neck. "I know everything will be all right. It's common for lads his age to play up on occasion."

Even as the words left Ginger's mouth, she felt a stab of uncertainty. She'd known Scout had been unhappy at Kingswell Academy but had written it off as his nerves and him not liking change. She and

Basil had been confident he'd adjust over time, as most lads do, but clearly he had not.

Ginger pushed back at an uncomfortable feeling of failure. Things had been going so well with Scout —he was always such a cheery, delightful lad, even whilst amid hard-living. Certainly, he'd grown sullener and moodier as he'd got older, and if her student-doctor friend Haley Higgins were around, Ginger was certain she would reassure her it was a matter of growing pains and not poor parenting.

Still, Ginger couldn't ignore a growing sense of guilt.

After a final soft squeeze, Ginger released Boss and headed towards the staircase in the entranceway. She suddenly needed to check on baby Rosa in the nursery on the floor above.

"Oh, there you are!" Ginger said brightly as she stepped toward the crib where her dark haired daughter lay playing with her toes. Carefully lifting the babe into her arms, she turned to the sturdy nurse, Abby Green, who was busy folding nappies.

"Little Rosa's a delight, madam," Nanny said. "Barely cries except to let me know she's hungry."

Both Ginger and Basil had good dispositions, so the news wasn't surprising. Having one happy and healthy child was a balm to her soul, but it didn't erase the unease and upset she carried over Scout.

"It's almost time for a feed, madam," Nanny said. "Grace is bringing up a warmed bottle of milk."

"Jolly good," Ginger said. "I'll stay to feed her."

Grace, one of the Hartigan House maids, arrived shortly, and Ginger took her position in the rocking chair, cuddling her little daughter in her arms. She couldn't help but smile at the round green eyes that stared up at her as her little rosebud lips worked the rubber nipple of the glass bottle.

The room brought a sense of peace and well-being with the nursery walls painted green on the top and wallpapered on the bottom with a pattern of big pink bows. And the ray of sun shining through the windows—how could one not be filled with hope and joy whilst rocking the child? Eventually, Rosa tired of the bottle, and Ginger handed the baby over to the nurse to do the back-patting duties. As much as Ginger wanted to stay, her heart was too bothered by Scout's plight to take mental refuge for long.

Checking her wristwatch before heading down the staircase, Ginger wondered what was taking Basil. Surely, he should arrive soon? Passing the sitting room doors, Ginger spotted Ambrosia having tea with Felicia, who, since her marriage to Charles,

Lord Davenport-Witt, resided on the other side of Mallowan Court, a cul-de-sac graced with manor-like houses made of limestone and brick.

Splendid! Just the diversion Ginger needed whilst waiting for Basil to return.

"Ginger, darling," Felicia said. She wore a pale green chiffon frock with a lace collar and handker-chief hemline. Her dark hair was cut short to the base of her neck with the edge growing longer as it reached her chin, a jewelled hairpin keeping the fringe from falling across her face. Emerald teardrop clip-on earrings hung from dainty lobes. "You look distressed," she continued. "Is everything all right?"

"It's Scout," Ginger said with a sigh.

Ambrosia, on hearing Ginger's upset was merely due to the lad who'd come to the family as an "urchin", noticeably relaxed. The matronly dowager's straight posture defied her age, thanks to her dedication to her corset. Grey hair was pulled into a bun, and her wrinkled face remained free of make-up, which she still considered a vice of those of ill repute, an opinion she'd been forced to relin-quish as Ginger and Felicia were fans of the face paint. She held the silver handle of her walking stick with crooked fingers well adorned with rings possessed of large gems. "Have a cup of tea, dear," she said. She rang the bell which quickly produced a maid.

"Bring Mrs. Reed a teacup," Ambrosia said, to which the maid curtsied and hurried away to do the dowager's bidding.

Ginger claimed her favourite chair and allowed herself a moment to relax. The sitting room was amongst the most comfortable in the house, with wingback chairs and a matching settee facing the stone fireplace. A John William Waterhouse painting called *The Mermaid* hung over the mantel, a fire burned in the hearth, and nearby was a vacant dog bed. The floor was warmed with a thick and ornate Persian carpet, and the tall windows were draped with light sheer curtains. The wireless was turned on low, and "Ain't She Sweet" played in the background.

The maid arrived with a third setting, and Ginger helped herself to a hot cup of tea.

"Do tell us what's happening with Scout," Felicia said. "More difficulties at school?"

"Worse than that, I'm afraid," Ginger said after a sip. "He's run away."

Felicia sat up straight, nearly spilling her tea. "No!"

"To the circus."

Ambrosia's teacup rattled against the saucer. "Are you quite serious? *The circus?*"

Ginger thought her former grandmother-in-law was about to faint. At her age, and no one liked to think about just how old Ambrosia was, what one member of society thought about another was of prime importance.

"I'm afraid so, Grandmama," Ginger said. "I've received word from Marvin Elliot telling me so."

"Marvin, Scout's cousin?" Felicia enquired. "Isn't he in the navy?"

"He was," Ginger said with a sigh. "He's been discharged and it appears has joined the circus as well."

Ambrosia snorted softly. "I'll never hear the end of it now. You know how word spreads. We'll be the laughing stock. I knew you—"

Ginger held up a palm, shooting Ambrosia a look of warning. "Please, don't say anything you'll regret later."

"I'm quite capable of holding my tongue when need be," Ambrosia said with tight lips. She proved her point by sipping her tea and glancing away.

"Actually," Felicia started, "Charles and I have tickets. We're going to the opening tonight."

Ambrosia glared at her granddaughter. "I

thought such affairs were intended to placate the lower classes."

"Oh no," Felicia said. "All classes love the circus. Why shouldn't we enjoy elephants' splendour and the breathtaking spectacles? I'd argue that our class suffers the most from boredom. I expect to see several people from our social circle there."

Ambrosia's shoulders folded. "Oh, heavens." Then, with a new resolve, "Let us talk of other matters, shall we?"

"Charles Lindberg landed in Paris." Ginger said. "The first solo flight over the Atlantic. The papers are full of it."

"In one of those flying sardine tins?" Ambrosia said in disbelief. "You wouldn't catch me dead in one of those."

"It's an engineering feat, Grandmama," Felicia said.

"Whatever it is," Ambrosia returned defiantly, "it's not natural."

"Speaking of a Charles," Felicia started. "My Charles is home for a few days." The look of relief on her face was evident.

"He does work rather a lot," Ambrosia said, "for someone born to privilege."

Ginger was the only one of the three who understood the true nature of her brother-in-law's "work". Felicia and Ambrosia believed him to be overly involved in the goings-on at the House of Lords when, in fact, Charles, like Ginger had been, was involved with the secret service. Political concerns in England were of particular concern, such as the recent looting of the British consulate by some Chinese in Nanjing, where two British civilians had been killed. And fears of "The Red Menace of Communism" were now causing all kinds of tension in the political circles at home and abroad.

"At least you have us to keep you company," Ginger said.

"I do, and for that, I'm grateful, but it's not only that. It's—" Felicia paused, her gaze lingering on her cup.

"What is it?" Ginger asked kindly.

Felicia glanced up and, looking sheepish, answered, "It's Burton."

"The butler?" Ginger said.

"Yes. He's an entirely different creature when Charles is away. He ignores me, pretending to be hard of hearing, though his ears undergo a miraculous cure when Charles is around.

"He's the *butler,*" Ambrosia said, bemused. "Surely, he should be the one having a problem with

25

you. It's your prerogative to let him go if he displeases you."

"But he's been with Charles for donkey's years," Felicia said with a mild whine. "I'm new to the situation. I feel Burton resents my coming into my position so quickly."

"Some lady was bound to eventually," Ginger said. "But I understand how you must feel like you're in the middle and not wanting to put Charles into an awkward situation. His butler will warm to you, eventually."

"I do hope so," Felicia said. "At least Daphne has adapted nicely. She's actually an exceptionally good lady's maid."

"Why are you not calling her by her surname as is proper?" Ambrosia asked.

"The maid's name is Daphne Cook," Felicia explained, "and calling her Cook would just be confusing when there's a cook in the kitchen."

"I've always called my maid Lizzie," Ginger said. "I think one can do whatever one is comfortable with." She checked her wristwatch and rose to her feet. "I need to check on the baby before Basil gets here. We're going together to pick up Scout."

4

*B*asil was tempted to head south on Millbank in his green '22 Austin towards Vauxhall Bridge and fetch Scout himself, but he knew he'd never hear the end of it if he didn't do as he'd said he would and pick Ginger up first.

Besides, Ginger was the most level-headed lady he knew, even when her emotions were sparked. It wasn't like Scout was in mortal danger. And if any lad could fend for himself, it was Scout.

Basil had driven this route a thousand times, along Victoria Street, up Grosvenor Place, the left onto Knightsbridge, continuing onto Brompton Road and towards South Kensington. With his mind on Ginger, he imagined her caring for the baby, making sure little Rosa was safe and comfortable while she waited for him. The vision made his heart melt. He'd loved no one as much as he loved and adored his wife, but little Rosa had simply captured his heart with his dark hair and her mother's green eyes.

Scout landed in an entirely different category, coming into Basil's life as a boy of eleven when Basil had married Ginger. It didn't mean he loved Scout less—because the lad had captured his heart as well —it just felt different.

And if anyone harmed the lad at the circus or elsewhere, Basil would be the first to come to his defence and give the bloke involved a thorough beating!

Basil's mind was so captured with thoughts of his family, he missed seeing the horse and cart pull away from the kerb. Basil's quick reflexes had him tugging at the steering wheel, jerking the motorcar out of the way just in time.

He shook a fist at the startled driver, and if Basil hadn't been in a hurry, he would've stopped the man and cautioned him to pay more careful attention to other road users.

As it was, he wanted Ginger to wait for him to make the drive across the Thames. Ginger was excellent at many things, but driving wasn't one of them, though she'd argue the fact if one presented it to her.

Basil pulled into the lane that led to the garage in the back garden of Hartigan House. The gardener, Clement, approached.

"Good afternoon, sir. Mrs. Reed had asked me to ready the Crossley." He nodded toward the exquisite pearly-white machine that he kept polished.

"That won't be necessary," Basil said. "I've come to fetch her."

Opposite the garage was a small stable that housed two horses, Basil's Arabian, Sir Blackwell, and Ginger's incredibly beautiful shimmering blond Akhal-Teke called Goldmine. Scout used to take care of the two geldings with Clement's oversight.

Clement, seeing Basil gaze at the stall, reassured Basil. "The horses are brushed and fed, sir. Could use a riding, though."

Basil ducked his chin in acknowledgement. He and Ginger tried to go out twice a week, but recent weather had been too inclement, and he'd been busy at work. "Master Scout is returning soon," Basil said. "The two of us will go out then."

Inside, he found Ginger in the entrance hall, accepting her spring coat from Pippins. "I saw you drive up," she said. "I'm ready to go."

. . .

Scout stared up at a work crew putting up the final riggings of the high wire that stretched between two scaffold structures. From where he was standing in the centre ring, the tiny platforms they worked from seemed impossibly high and ridiculously tiny. Scout felt dizzy just looking up at the three men pulling ropes, tightening bolts, and fastening colourful flags. The striped, white-and-blue ceiling of the tent only added to the feeling of vertigo, and Scout had to look away after only a few moments.

A man stood at the base of one of the main poles, shouting up at the work crew. "That's it, lads!" In his early thirties, he had jet-black hair slicked back behind his ears. He wore grey wool trousers, a waistcoat, boots, and a collarless green shirt with rolled-up sleeves. An unlit cigar stuck out of his mouth, and he chewed it as he pointed towards one end of the high-wire assembly. "Get the wire as taut as you can this time!"

Not known for his shyness, Scout took a few steps towards the man and pointed his chin back up at the high wire. "I'd like to meet the person that walks that thing. I know I could never do it."

"And I wouldn't advise it neither," the man returned with a chuckle. "But as far as meetin' the poor sod who has to walk that wire every night, well . . . you just have."

Scout's eyebrows jumped in surprise. "Really?"

"Horace Rhimes is the name, son." The man was lean and muscular, with a sharp jaw and deep-set eyes. He stuck out his hand and continued, "Otherwise known as The Lord of the High Wire. And I don't just walk it; I ride unicycles across it, and if I'm not doin' that, I'm balancin' on a chair havin' a cup of tea an' readin' the sports section."

"Crikey," said Scout, as he took the offered hand. "Very pleased to meet you, Mr. Rhimes. They call me Scout."

"Scout, eh?" Horace Rhimes said. "Good name. You're one of the newly hired crew, are yer?"

"Er, not yet. My cousin Marvin works 'ere, and he just went to fetch someone for me to talk to. I'm 'opin' to get on."

"Ah, the circus' call has reached your ears, has it?" The wire walker nodded with a small smile. "I heard the call when I was about your age. Me and my sister Ethel."

"You perform together?"

"We did." Mr. Rhimes stared upwards with a note of sadness in his eyes, but before a story could follow, Scout's attention was captured by a slight figure wearing white and black face paint. The fellow waved him over.

"You're a mime?" Scout said.

The youthful fellow nodded. He wore a black-and-white striped shirt, black trousers with braces, and a black cap. White face paint ending in the sharp outline of an oval covered his features and was accentuated by bright red lipstick, black tear drops, and thickly painted black eyebrows.

The mime placed his gloved hands on his hips, and scowled. Without saying a word, he pointed his finger in the air, raised his painted eyebrows, and opened his mouth as if struck by a brilliant new idea. He then leaned sideways and hunched his left shoulder. It looked to Scout as if Kiki was leaning on an invisible wall. The mime then reached into his pocket and pulled something out. Though his hand was empty, it seemed like Kiki was magically lifting a cigarette out of a cigarette holder. Then, the mime put the invisible gasper to his mouth and patted his pockets, searching for a lighter. Finding none, he reached behind Scout's left ear and, somehow, pulled out an actual match, which he struck on the wooden seat behind him and lit the invisible cigarette. The mime took a long, exaggerated drag while waving out the match and then exhaling an imaginary plume of smoke out of the left side of his painted mouth. All of this was done while still leaning on the invisible wall.

"Cor!" Scout shouted, giving the mime sincere applause. "That was splendid!"

Scout had never seen anything like this performance before.

"It's called miming," the mime said, straightening up. "I'm Kiki."

Scout was surprised at how young Kiki sounded; his voice was barely deeper than Scout's own.

"Amazin'! Are you a clown or somefin'?

"We mimes don't like to be called clowns," Kiki cautioned. "A clown is someone who acts in a silly fashion to make people laugh. A mime is an actor who makes props out of thin air and acts out in mime."

"I'm Scout, by the way."

Kiki ducked his chin in acknowledgement. "Are you looking for work here too?" Kiki asked.

Scout nodded enthusiastically. "I'm 'opin' to."

"I hope you can," Kiki said. "I've only been here a short time, but I already feel like I'm family."

Scout had indeed already felt like this environment suited him more than high society. He found the scent of dirt, sawdust, and animal sweat comforting. If he were honest with himself, Scout had felt like an outcast his whole life. Perhaps here, surrounded by other outcasts, he would find a place where he truly belonged.

"Dash it all!" An angry voice boomed from the main entrance of the tent. It came from a tall man in his forties who wore a long, waxed moustache that curled into circles on his cheeks, which were now reddened with his fury. "Haven't you got that finished yet? You still have to set up the trapeze and all the netting!" He held up his arm and pointed to his wristwatch.

"They can't read your watch from up there," Horace Rhimes shouted in response, "You need to lay off him. There's still four hours to go till openin'. It's when the crews are rushed that accidents happen. You should know better than that by now, I'd say."

"No excuse for faffing about," the man shot back, glaring as he tugged on his red waistcoat.

Marvin had joined them and Scout asked him, "Is that the circus owner?"

"No, but 'e wishes 'e was, I'll bet," Marvin said. "The owner lives in Cornwall. I've never met the bloke, but if I ever did, I'd let 'im know that 'e picked a right miserable man to manage 'is circus."

"That's the ringmaster," Kiki said. "He's got the job of managing the circus, and if he catches us standing about, it'll be our jobs." With that, Kiki slipped behind the stands, out of sight. Scout wondered if he and Marvin should be doing the same.

Marvin's gaze followed the mime's departure. "Always someone new joinin' the circus. It's 'ard to keep up."

Just then a large horse-drawn cart carrying a load of brightly painted boxes of various sizes entered through the main entrance. Scout looked twice at the two men sitting on the driver's bench behind the two chestnut mares. At first, he thought his eyes were playing tricks on him. The man holding the reins was dressed in overalls and wore a bright blue woollen cap, but Scout was struck by the man's face, completely covered in thick, long brown hair. There was not an inch of skin seen from chin to forehead. It was as if a shaggy-haired animal had donned work clothes and learned to drive a cart. The hair was arranged so that from the bottom of the man's eyes downward, it was combed to the sides like a great flowing beard that went to the top of his chest. Hair from the tip of his nose and beyond was combed back and over his head.

The fellow sitting next to him wore similar clothes, but what stuck out about him was that he was so small. Scout was small for his age, but even he would tower over this man, who, besides his diminutive stature, had all the signs of a full-grown man, including a beard and a weather-wrinkled face.

Marvin elbowed him. "Not polite to stare, squirt."

"Yeah, sorry." Scout forced his gaze to move about the tent where men and animals bustled about.

"That's Dmytro Petrenko," Marvin said, making himself look busy by tying a rope to a pole. "Better known as Dmytro the dog-faced man from the Ukraine. The little bloke there is Prince Natukunda of Uganda. The tallest man of the Zambezi tribe."

"The *tallest* man?"

"Yep. Now, 'elp me tie this rope properly. And don't stare Bancroft in the eyes."

"Who's Bancroft?"

"The ringmaster. Believe me, yer don't wanna get on 'is bad side."

s Ginger and Basil headed through Chelsea and alongside Battersea Park, Ginger's mind was pinpointed on Scout and how she would give him a piece of her mind when they found him.

"I want to grab him and drag him home," she said. "It's not my style, but perhaps that's what he responds to. If he's going to revert to his street-life behaviour, then he needs the same kind of discipline his uncle used to dish out."

Basil patted Ginger's leg. "Now, now. It's not like you to make a scene. The Ginger I know is rather subtle."

Ginger sighed. It was true. Her days during the Great War had taught her to keep a tight rein on her emotions and keep her feelings from reflecting in her eyes.

"Motherhood has ruined me, Basil," she said. "I've turned into mush."

"Hardly ruined, love," Basil said with a smile. "Enhanced."

In the distance, the tips of the circus tents came into view, the striped canvas billowing slightly in the breeze.

The grounds around the tents were busy with men scurrying about and motor lorries parked here and there as the circus supplies were unloaded. Basil parked on one of the side streets, and as they walked closer to the main entrance, they were greeted with a large, colourful sign: COME ONE, COME ALL!

The air was tinged with the unpleasant smell of sweaty, nervous anticipation—both human and animal.

The inside was a beehive of activity, with construction workers creating sets, animals being led about, and food vendors getting their kiosks ready. Nearby, a tall man with a long waxed and curled moustache appeared to be arguing with a shorter man partially dressed in a clown outfit, his pantaloons held out from his thin waist by a wire, making him look like he'd stepped into a life-size, upside down lampshade. His nose was naturally large, soft, and needing no artificial costume enhancement.

"You may be *King* of the Clowns," the tall man said, "but that still makes you a nobody. What I say goes!"

The King of the Clowns pointed a finger at the tall man's chest. "You're going too far, Bancroft—" The rest of his speech was lost in the commotion of a group of acrobats practising cartwheels and backflips in the newly spread-out sawdust.

As the man Ginger now knew as Mr. Bancroft stormed away, he bumped into a man of average height who had an unfortunate medical condition, causing hair to grow all over his face. Her friend Haley Higgins had told her about hypertrichosis, also known as werewolf syndrome, a condition characterised by excessive growth of bodily hair. It was common for circuses to exploit people with rare conditions and birth defects as spectacles to be gawked at and ridiculed, which Ginger found extremely distasteful.

Mr. Bancroft spewed, "Get out of my way, you hairy blighter!" then froze when he noticed Ginger and Basil watching. He waved his hands at the half man-half clown, who jogged over to greet them.

Ginger bit her lip to keep from grinning at his get-up.

"Hello," he said. "The show don't start until six."

Basil slipped a hand into his pocket and produced his police card. "I'm Chief Inspector Reed. And who would you be?"

"Leonard Quill. Head clown."

"Mr. Quill," Basil continued. "We're looking for a lad, short in stature, with dirty-blond hair who goes by the name of Scout. He might be here visiting his cousin Marvin Elliott."

Mr. Quill hooked his thumbs around the braces that held up his pantaloons. "Marvin, yeah, I know him. Sorry, I haven't met a lad called Scout."

"Where would we find Mr. Elliot?" Ginger asked.

"He's assisting the head animal trainer," the man said. "Singh's his name, straight out of India." He pointed to a flap at the back of the tent. "Head that way. You'll hear the animals making a fuss. They always get excited the first night at a new place. Your man Marvin will probably be there, or someone will know how to find him."

Ginger and Basil thanked Mr. Quill and left the main tent through the door flap he'd indicated.

"I wanna kick him in his long-legged shin!"

The outburst came from a short fellow, a dwarf with dark skin, who had joined the man with hyper-trichosis. Ginger immediately recalled a dwarf named Armand that she'd met in Belgium during the war. He was a courageous man who'd helped smuggle people across German lines into the Netherlands.

The man with the facial hair shrugged at the smaller man. "He's boss," he said with a thick Slavic accent. "Nothing we can do but what he says and collect our pay."

"Pay! Pittance!"

"I know, Prince," the man returned, "but it is place to sleep and food in belly."

"The chimps eat better than us."

Basil cleared his throat, and the two men jumped. "Excuse us," the small man called Prince said.

Ginger smiled, hoping to disarm the startled men. "We're looking for a lad called Scout. Have you seen him?"

"Scout," Prince said with a stiff nod. "He could be anywhere."

The hairy man pointed. "I'd go that way, past the clown changing rooms."

"Thank you," Ginger said.

Clearly, they were headed in the right direction, as clowns were suddenly everywhere. Red noses, painted faces, red curly wigs. A shy mime darted out of sight the moment Ginger caught his gaze.

The King of Clowns had been correct when he'd said they'd hear the animals making a fuss. The screech of monkeys, roar of tigers, and the trumpeting of elephants grew louder with each step they took. Ginger grabbed Basil's arm.

"I feel like we've stepped into the jungle."

"Hopefully Scout hasn't turned into Tarzan," Basil returned.

Ginger immediately imagined the *Jungle Book* boy, Mowgli, with Scout's toothy grin and blond, unruly hair.

Oh mercy.

6

Scout—wearing a pair of wellingtons, a set of old clothes Marvin had found for him, and a cotton flat cap—followed his cousin past the tents and several hastily constructed wooden sheds, all the while trying to dodge the work crews who hustled to get the work done.

Following Marvin, Scout asked, "Where are we going?"

"To see Singh."

"Sing?" Scout said, his voice cracking. He hated when that happened, and it happened a lot lately. Marvin shot him an amused look, but took pity on him, saving a teasing for another day.

"The head animal trainer. He's the chap who'll

give you a job. Tarjeet Singh's from India. They practically grow up with wild animals there."

Scout had just finished rereading Rudyard Kipling's *The Jungle Book*. It made him dream of going to India and having an exotic adventure. India might as well be the moon. The circus was as close to India as he'd ever get. He scampered after Marvin with a skip in his step.

"Chimps," Marvin said. He nodded to the other workers who were seeing to the feed and water.

The chimpanzees pointed at Scout, chatting and guffawing as if Scout were the one on exhibition instead of the other way around.

"Hey, fellows," he said with a smile. "How's the battle?"

"They only understand Punjabi," Marvin said as he tipped Scout's cap off his head.

Scout stooped to pick up the fallen cap. "Very funny."

"Where's Singh?" Marvin asked a man with a bag of feed on his shoulder.

The man grunted under his load. "Elephants."

Scout caught his breath at the thought of the elephants. This was what he was waiting for!

Scout felt like he'd stepped through the pages of a fantastic adventure novel, following Marvin as he traipsed past small tents with intriguing signs: Cedric the Snake Charmer, Priscilla the Contortionist, and the Strongest Man on Earth. He pinched himself. "Ow." No, this was real.

"A circus barker announces each act," Marvin explained. "Folk pay for tickets to look at what's inside."

When they finally rounded a corner and came to the elephants, all Scout could do was stare open-mouthed. He'd seen elephants from a distance already earlier that day and photographs before that, but seeing them up close in real life was the berries. Five grown elephants and two calves stood in an outdoor steel enclosure. The adults were chained by their back feet to large posts in the ground while the calves stood beside their mothers untethered. The musky smell of elephant dung and hay filled the air. The majestic, wrinkly, beautiful animals grabbed hay from a trough with their trunks and stuffed it into their mouths.

"Crikey!" Scout put a hand on the top of his head in amazement. "They're frightfully splendid!"

"The two babies are Coco and Scarlett," Marvin said. "I don't know which is which. This one . . ." he gestured grandly to the largest elephant in the row, "is the oldest at twenty-seven. 'Er name is Tulip."

Scout smiled at the name and said tentatively, "Hi, Tulip."

The animal turned her head from the trough and regarded Scout while she continued placidly chewing her meal. Scout couldn't keep his grin from stretching across his face. "She knows 'er name all right!"

"Of course she does," Marvin said.

Scout's face grew serious as he stared at Tulip's manacled back foot. "Why do they have to be chained?"

A heavily accented voice came from behind. "Can you imagine what those beasts could do if they decided they were having a bad day?" Scout turned to see an olive-skinned man wearing a white collarless shirt and a black turban.

"A pachyderm is a very gentle animal most of the time," the man continued as he leaned against the steel enclosure. "And they are terribly intelligent. I would choose Tulip over my brother Amar any time in a game of draughts."

Scout scrunched his face. "Draughts?"

"Oh yes, all these elephants can play draughts. They can play cricket too. Murdoch, the one on the end there, plays a harmonica." He grinned. "We're also thinking of starting our very own elephant cricket team here. Tulip can throw a ball accurately."

Scout couldn't tell if the man was being serious or pulling his leg.

"Naturally, we would need a few more elephants," the man continued with a chuckle, "but to answer your question, we have to keep them chained because it would be too dangerous, for us, and for them, to let them just wander about."

"I guess so," Scout said, but it still saddened him somehow as he stared at the manacles.

"Especially if they have been drinking."

Scout's head snapped back to look at the Indian man. "What do you mean?"

"Tulip especially likes to have a nip once in a while," the man replied. At the sound of her name, Tulip raised her trunk in the air and let out a short bellow, making Scout laugh.

"Scout, this is Mr. Tarjeet Singh," Marvin said, breaking in. "He trains the elephants and the chimpanzees. Mr. Singh, this is my cousin Scout."

"Ah, pleased to meet you, young man." Instead of shaking hands, Mr. Singh bowed slightly with his palms pressed together in front of him.

"Good to meet you, sir, but what do you mean about Tulip drinking?" Scout asked.

"Tulip likes to enjoy a little drop of spirits, from time to time. A little-known fact about elephants is that some of them can grow to love the taste of alcohol. When Tulip was with the previous circus, the trainer, who was a known drunk, used to come in after the show and share his bottle of whisky with her. Tulip is as calm and gentle an elephant as you'll ever meet, but she does like her whisky."

"Blimey!" Scout said. He'd seen plenty of street drunks in his time but had never met an animal that liked the booze.

"Tulip never gets aggressive," Mr. Singh added, "though she does do silly things after a nip or two. But . . ." He held up a finger. "Only the more expensive brands. She will turn her nose, er, trunk, up, if you'll pardon the expression, at anything less than a twelve-year-old single malt. If you give her enough of that, she'll get a little tipsy. I sometimes share a drink with her after a particularly good show, just to reward her, or even before a show to calm her nerves, just not very much."

Scout stared at Tulip. Who had ever heard of such a thing?

"Scout's lookin' to join us for a while, Mr. Singh," Marvin said, putting his hand on Scout's shoulder. "I was wonderin' if you might 'ave an openin'."

"I'm really good wiv animals!" Scout said. "I 'ad jobs before, takin' care of 'em. They all seem to like me."

Mr. Singh put a hand to his chin. "I wouldn't mind having someone to clean the monkey cages. They make an awful mess. Also feeding the elephants here and picking up after . . ."

"I'll do it! I'll do anyfin' you ask," Scout exclaimed and then grew serious, "Oh, forgive me, sir, I interrupted."

"My, my," Mr. Singh said with a look of interest. "Someone has taught you manners, even if you momentarily forget them. I haven't seen that around here very much, especially not from someone as young as you."

"Yes, sir," was all Scout could think of to say.

Mr. Singh reached for a dirty shovel and handed it to Scout. "Here you go, Scout." He pointed to one elephant who'd chosen that moment to leave a big dung pile. "There's a bin out the back. Be careful not to get stepped on."

"Yes, sir," Scout said. He held his breath against the stench then carefully stepped to the back of the pen, keeping his eyes on those big round feet.

"You'll need to use that barrow over there." Marvin pointed to a rickety wooden wheelbarrow sitting next to a rack of shovels and brooms and a wooden step ladder. "Grab yerself a shovel and a stiff-bristled broom."

"What are those big buckets for?" Scout asked.

"That's for washin' the elephants. I don't fink you're quite ready for that yet. Let's see how you do wiv cleanin' up their droppin's first." Marvin waved his hand vaguely at the many piles of elephant dung —round, grey-brown droppings the size of a football —lying on the hard-packed dirt.

Tulip, along with the rest of the elephants, stood idly all on one side of the enclosure. Tulip regarded Marvin and Scout with mild curiosity out of one large copper-coloured eye while chewing on fresh hay from a nearby feeder trough.

"The job's simple," Marvin said. "Use the shovel to put it all in the wheelbarrow and then dump each load into that big steel bin over there. Use the broom to sweep up the smaller bits." Chuckling, he slapped Scout on the back. "'Ave fun!" He then left Scout alone in the enclosure with the huge beasts.

Overwhelmed to be alone with such large beasts, Scout froze on the spot. Tulip was nearest to him, and once again Scout got the feeling she was sizing him up.

"It's all right, girl," Scout whispered dryly as he

awkwardly waved one hand at her, then tentatively, he stepped backwards to fetch the shovel and the wheelbarrow. Soon he got into a rhythm of shovelling and depositing the dung into the barrow and transporting it to the bin and returning, all the while keeping one eye on the elephants.

After about half an hour, his arms and back ached, and he stretched out. He closed his eyes, forgetting momentarily where he stood. A second later, he felt a light nudge on his shoulder, which made him quickly turn around.

He hadn't realised he'd got so close to Tulip, and his heart leapt into his throat. But his fright all but disappeared when Tulip grasped his cap with her long trunk and deftly placed it on her own head.

Scout protested, "Hey!" He couldn't stop a bout of laughter at the ridiculous sight of the small cap sitting atop her huge skull.

He shyly took a few steps forward and carefully held out his hand. When Tulip showed no signs of aggression, he stretched out on his tiptoes and placed his palm on the flat space between her huge, wrinkled eyes, patting the rough, dry skin.

"You're a clever girl, aren't you?"

As though affirming his statement as a well-known fact, Tulip blinked slowly.

Scout stepped back when he saw she was raising her trunk. Had he irritated her? She gently placed the end of her snout on the top of his head as though mimicking his own gesture. She then started gently patting his head in the same way. Tulip was communicating with him!

"Yeah, I'm pretty clever too, even if I do say so meself," he returned with a smile.

The next moment, she stepped back, and to Scout's astonishment, she lowered her head as she bent one knee. She tapped his right leg with her trunk, bending it upwards to form a step.

Scout stared at her with astonishment. "You want me to get on?"

When Tulip didn't move from that position, Scout reached up and grabbed the front folds of her huge ears and stepped on to her outstretched trunk. She raised her head, and he scrambled up the rest of the way, turning to sit with his knees nestled in right behind her ears. He grabbed his hat and put it back on his head.

Scout whispered, "Wahoo!" as Tulip took a few steps backwards and forwards again, as far as her manacled leg would let her. "I am Mowgli!" Scout exclaimed. "I'm the legend of the jungle. I'm the prince of the Indian forests!"

Just then, he heard Mr. Singh talking to Marvin in the corridor.

"Uh-oh," Scout whispered.

Tulip seemed to understand as she once again lowered her head and formed her trunk so Scout could quickly scramble down. He then snatched up the broom and swept.

"Good work," Mr. Singh said as he and Marvin peeked in. "It's looking cleaner already."

After they were gone, Scout leaned against the broom handle and grinned at his gigantic new friend.

7

*T*hey spotted Scout before he saw them, his thin back hunched over as he scooped foul-smelling elephant dung into a bucket. That wasn't what had Ginger holding her breath though. It was the nearness of the five-ton, flat-footed animals who could stomp the life out of her son at any moment!

The small herd seemed to notice her before her son did, their large leathery ears flapping, their round inquisitive eyes staring. One of them raised its trunk, a perfect moniker, as it was the size of a large oak branch. The elephant swung it from side to side.

Before Ginger could stop herself, she shouted his name, "Scout!"

Startled, Scout dropped his shovel as he turned,

stepping back. "What?" he said, unable to hide the surprise on his face. "What are you doing 'ere?"

Ginger immediately noticed he'd dropped his *H*, but that was the least of her concerns right at that moment.

"You've had us worried sick," she said. "Now, enough of this nonsense. Come, we're going home."

Scout threw his shoulders back in defiance. "I'm not goin' back to that school, and you can't make me!"

"Now, Scout," Basil said. "Let's go home, and we'll talk it over."

"I am 'ome. Wiv me cousin."

Ginger's eyebrows came together in annoyed puzzlement. "Why are you talking like that? It's not who you are anymore."

"But it is who I am, madam," Scout said. "These are my family now."

Madam? Scout had been calling her "Mum" for two years. But claiming they were no longer his family was a real stab in the heart.

"This is ridiculous," she said. "Scout, you must come home *now*. We can talk about all of this, then.

"You must come home *now!*"

Ginger spun at the mimicking voice. Behind them stood two clowns, dressed in bright costumes of stripes and dots, faces painted, making them unrecognisable.

The second one taunted, "Go home, posh mummy's boy!"

They laughed then scurried away like troublesome vermin. Scout's face grew red with embarrassment.

"I'm not posh and never will be!" He turned his back on Ginger and Basil, but not in time to hide a sniffle as he wiped his nose with the back of his sleeve.

"Scout?" Ginger said softly. "We're your family."

"Not no more," Scout said with a quiver. After a breath, he said firmly, "Please go."

Ginger took a step, but Basil grabbed her arm, holding her back. He led her out of the elephant pen, saying quietly, "Let's leave him for now. A man needs to prove his point. It's not like he's in any danger here."

"No danger?" Ginger protested, scowling at the clowns as they walked by. "He's taking care of *elephants*." She shook her head, "And he's not a man, he's a *boy*."

"These elephants are used to being around people. They're not wild, Ginger. Think of them as you do Boss, only much, much larger."

Ginger thought Basil's analogy was a stretch but loved him for trying.

They worked their way back to the big tent, which was now empty but for a few workers. Just before they made it to the main entrance, the tall man with the extreme moustache stepped in front of them. As if he could use a week's worth of sleep, his skin was pale and dark rings encircled his eyes. His gaze travelled from Ginger's face to her toes in a way that made her want to slap the moustache off his face.

"Excuse me," he said, "but I thought you were told that the gates don't open until tonight."

"I'm Chief Inspector Basil Reed," Basil said, once again producing his card. "We were looking for a runaway. And who might you be?"

"I'm Luther Bancroft, ringmaster." His lips formed a crooked smile as he extended long fingers towards Ginger. "And who is this pretty lady?"

Ginger forced civility and accepted the man's hand. "I'm Mrs. Reed, but I'm known by many in London as Lady Gold."

Ginger rarely threw her title around, a privilege she had put aside when she married Basil, but something about this man made her want to put him in his place.

"Lady Gold?" he said with a raised brow. "Of Lady Gold Investigations?"

"Yes," Ginger said. "You've heard of my office?"

"Indeed, your reputation precedes you. No doubt your wily detective talents have produced the lad you're looking for?"

"We've found what we've come for," Basil said stiffly. "Please excuse us. I'm certain you have plenty to do before tonight."

"Opening night is always busy, but also the most exciting," Mr. Bancroft said. He played with the tip of one side of his waxy moustache. "Will you be coming? We get all manner of the elite and the working classes together. You'll fit right in."

Ginger huffed as they returned to Basil's motor-car. "The nerve of that man. Just who does he think he is?"

Basil opened the passenger door for Ginger. "He's a man who's stuck in a life he detests," he said. "He's to be pitied."

A FEW HOURS LATER, Scout and Marvin headed to the big tent to catch the show's beginning. Scout's emotions were still a storm, a whirlwind of resentment and . . . something else he couldn't quite identify. Not often in his life had someone come looking for him out of concern for his safety, and it confused him. And seeing Lady Gold had made Scout decide to go back to the name he had known her by when they first met. Mrs. Reed seemed too formal, and Mum didn't seem to fit anymore—he felt off-balance in ways he couldn't explain. Not only that, but he was also feeling the effects of a lighter wallet. He'd grown used to the three square meals provided by Kingswell, and though he'd been busy gawking at the spectacles of circus life, intoxicated by the sights and sounds and his new friendship with Tulip, the food stalls reminded him of his growing hunger.

"I want some peanuts," he announced.

Marvin frowned. "That's for the customers. It's not free. There's food for the workers in the mess tent."

Scout had proudly presented his wallet, which Marvin was quick to slap away. "Don't be an idiot waving that about, or yer won't have it for long."

Chastised, Scout slipped the wallet into his pocket, only to present it again. "I got money, Marvin." Scout scampered away from his cousin and bought not only a paper bag of roasted peanuts from the vendor standing beside a trolley but also a stick of candy floss.

Finding Marvin sitting on the bottom row in one of the main seating sections, he extended his hand. "Want some?"

"You eat all that, and you'll be sick," Marvin said, though his admonishment didn't keep him from dropping his dirty mitt into the bag and scooping up a generous portion.

Scout gawked at the hundreds of exuberant spectators. As far as he could tell, they came from all walks of life and social class, distinguished by their clothing, how they held themselves, and who they sat with. The lower class—often given tickets to ensure the tent was filled each night—wore dirty rags for clothes, and some didn't even have shoes on their feet. The middle class looked clean and proper, with cheerful expressions that belonged to those with full stomachs. Even the elite were represented, the ladies with lace and frills and the gentlemen with stiff collars, all with their chins up and noses in the air. How had he ever believed he could be one of them? He almost pitied the children, trapped in such narrow confines of protocol and class distinction, yet, unlike him, they knew where they belonged.

Mr. Bancroft, the ringmaster, in his striped trousers, black, long-tailed jacket, and oversized top hat ran to the centre of the ring, a bright light following him like the Star of Bethlehem.

He lifted a megaphone to his lips, hidden by his mammoth moustache, and sang, "Ladies and gentlemen, The Flying Finch Sisters!"

Scout lost his appetite. His stomach dropped as he watched the death-defying trapeze acrobatics of these courageous ladies.

"Blimey," he muttered.

When the act was over, he let out a breath of relief. Though a net was held by many circus clowns, Scout hadn't wanted to see anyone fall. The clowns entertained the crowd between acts. Marvin had pointed out Leonard Quill, the King of Clowns, who had an unbelievably round girth and wore enormously oversized shoes. His antics made Scout laugh until the lemonade he was drinking blasted up his nose.

If the acrobatic ladies had made Scout's breath catch, Mr. Rhimes, the wire walker, almost had him blacking out, both with fear for the life of the man he'd met in person and awe at his tremendous talent. He performed unbelievable feats of balance on the high wire, including carrying a small stove in a wheelbarrow and then cooking an omelette.

Standing on a small platform attached to the

wire, he shouted, "Ladies and gentlemen! Do you see that little wooden wheelbarrow? Who will volunteer to ride across in it?"

A hush settled on the spectators. After a moment, a man wearing a bowler hat and a black suit shouted, "I will!"

Like a wave, a loud gasp rose from the crowd.

Horace Rhimes shouted back, "Do you believe in God?"

The man returned. "I've made my peace!"

Marvin murmured in Scout's ear. "'E works for the circus."

Scout felt a stab of disappointment, having got caught up in the ruse, but still, he was enthralled. As the man in the hat slowly climbed the ladder, the people jumped to their feet and then went wild as he was slowly trundled across the high wire by Mr. Rhimes. Loud shouts of "Hurrah, hurrah!" were heard throughout the tent.

When the act finished, Scout was elated. "I love the circus!"

Mr. Bancroft returned to the centre of the ring. "Ladies and gentlemen, coming to us from distant lands steeped in dark jungle and mystery, comes an act of truly mammoth proportion. My friends, you may have been told that the lion is the king of the jungle, but I tell you that there are creatures there that are so fearsome, so colossal that even the most terrible of the big cats wouldn't dare utter a single challenge. Dear citizens of London, ladies and gentlemen, boys and girls of all ages, I give you Mr. Singh and his Incredible Dancing Elephants!"

To the crowd's delight, Mr. Singh entered, riding on the back of a massive creature.

Scout pointed, recognising the beast. "That's Tulip!"

The other four adult elephants followed behind, each grasping the tail of the one before it with its trunk, giving the impression of a lumbering train. All the elephants had been dressed in beautiful, sequined head coverings that glittered in the spotlight as they slowly walked into the central ring.

Tulip stopped, bowed her head slightly as Mr. Singh, who wore a gold, sequinned turban and flouncy pantaloons, swung his legs over her head, slid down her trunk, and came to rest in its crook. He then lightly stepped off and onto the ground while the other elephants formed a semicircle around Tulip.

Scout's face hurt with all the smiling and laughing he'd done, and now, though he'd only just met them, he felt his chest burst with pride for the majestic animals.

Mr. Singh directed the smaller elephants to each stand on one of the heavier painted boxes laid out earlier by the dog-faced man and the dwarf. Standing in front of the first elephant in the line, he waved his baton. Amazingly, the elephant responded by balancing on its front two legs and lifting its rear legs into the air, performing a handstand! The other three elephants followed suit, and soon, all four were balancing on the box with their rear legs lifted high into the air.

"That's outstanding!" Scout said. In his excitement, he jumped to his feet. Marvin grinned as he grabbed Scout's arm and lowered him down. "The folks be'ind would like to see too."

While Mr. Singh was occupied with the four smaller adults, Scout watched Tulip swishing her huge ears and tail rapidly and bucking her head up and down.

"Is Tulip all right?" he asked.

Marvin's forehead buckled. "I'm not sure."

Mr. Bancroft stood outside the centre ring, his back turned as his attention was captured elsewhere.

Tulip lumbered over to the man, and for a scary moment, Scout thought she might ram into him, but instead, she stopped, then swung her trunk, and deftly knocked his tall top hat off his head.

The crowd erupted in laughter, and Scout joined in. Funny Tulip.

Mr. Bancroft's face was a mask of rage. Was it part of the act?

When he bent down and picked up his hat, Tulip reached out with her trunk and pushed him hard against his bottom. He fell face-first onto the sawdust.

The crowd roared with laughter even louder than before.

"Ha ha," Scout said to Marvin. "That's funnier than the clown act."

Marvin didn't seem to catch the joke. In fact, his face was as white as a sheet.

"What's the matter, Marvin?"

Marvin shook his head. "This ain't good, Scout. Not for anybody."

8

*L*ater, a small group gathered in the animal tents where someone had scrounged up food and drink. Scout was happy to help himself, though he had the sense to wait until the circus crew had gone first.

"I blame myself," Mr. Singh said.

"How can it be your fault," the King of Clowns asked.

With his make-up off, the King of Clowns—Mr. Quill—looked older than Scout would have guessed, perhaps in his mid-fifties with grey, slicked-back hair, a square jaw, big hands, and wide shoulders. Scout thought he could have been a boxer or a wrestler in his earlier years.

"Tonight was our first evening at this location,"

Mr. Singh said. "Tulip is my responsibility." He rolled his eyes in exaggerated frustration. "Sometimes, she gets a little nervous on opening night."

Prince Natukunda, the dwarf, poked the air with a stubby finger. "Uh-oh. Did she get into the whisky again?

"Indeed. My Glen Moray single malt. And I'm afraid she didn't 'get into it'."

Kiki, who remained in his mime costume, chuckled. "Are you saying you gave the elephant whisky?"

Mr. Singh's shoulders fell back defensively. "Just a little. It calms us both down."

Mr. Petrenko held up a half-empty bottle to his furry face and said in his thick Ukrainian accent, "Like medicine to help me smile and bow while people point. A few sips more after show even better. Helps me forget show."

He took another swig and then passed it to Scout. Eager to fit in, Scout took a quick drink. The unexpected burn caused him to grab at his throat, cough, and sputter.

Marvin slapped him on the back and took the bottle from him. "Hey! Yer need 'air on your chest before yer get to enjoy this."

"Yes, a little drink is all right," Mr. Singh said, "But you see, I was distracted for a moment by a commotion in the monkey cages, and I left the pen for a few minutes. I thought I'd put the bottle out of Tulip's reach, but that confounded long trunk! When I came back, she was happily pouring the rest of the bottle into her mouth."

"Tulip was tipsy!" Kiki squealed.

"It was so funny!" Scout said. "The ringmaster fell right on his face. The crowd loved it. Perhaps it should always be part of the show."

"I don't think our beloved ringmaster would share your sentiment," Mr. Quill said with a tinge of sarcasm.

"I'm not the kind who likes to speak ill of anyone," Mr. Singh said, "but Mr. Bancroft is a very nasty man."

Prince Natukunda nodded his short neck. "Very nasty,"

"He is bully," Mr. Petrenko said, stroking his face.

"Not just to people," Mr. Singh said, "but to animals as well."

Horace Rhimes, now dressed in the same clothes he was wearing when Scout had first met him, pulled up a chair. "You all know how I feel about that miserable swine."

"If everyone doesn't get on wiv 'im, why's'e the ringmaster?" Marvin asked.

"Yeah," Scout chimed in, feeling a bit dizzy but strangely bolder than usual. "And 'oo cares if 'e don't like what Tulip did? It's not like 'e can fire 'er."

Mr. Rhimes explained: "He is ringmaster because the owner, Mr. Sweeney, lives in Cornwall, which means he rarely comes to the circus unless it's near there."

Mr. Singh sighed. "Tulip may have been tipsy, but she has her reasons."

"What do you mean?" Kiki asked.

"He's brutal," Prince Natukunda said with a snarl. "I saw him pokin' the monkeys with a sharp stick and yellin' at the tigers while banging a metal cup loudly against the bars of their cages."

"I saw him kick members of dog troupe," Mr. Petrenko added.

"He's taken a whip to the elephants before," Mr. Singh said. "After tonight, he'll carry ill will towards Tulip, I'm sure of it."

A red-hot surge of anger rose in Scout's chest as recent memories of being pushed around and tormented at Kingswell by his classmates surfaced. And how many times had he run for his life whilst on the streets of London, a waif with only Marvin to protect him?

He shot to his feet and then caught himself before nearly toppling over. "I'll kill 'im if I ever see 'im doing that to 'er!" Everyone in the tent stared, and all Scout could hear was the hammering of his own heart in his chest.

Marvin patted his arm. "Stand down there, soldier. Tulip can look after 'erself. Now 'ow about we 'ead to bed. Tomorra comes early."

Before dawn the following day, Scout was abruptly pushed off his camp bed.

"Hey," Scout protested.

"Up, sleepyhead," Marvin said unapologetically. "What yer did fer the elephants yesterday, needs to be done with the chimps this morning. No shortage of dung in the circus."

At least Marvin had heated up the tea, which Scout drank before heading to the chimp cages.

"Hey, fella," Scout said as the large patriarch, Gonzo, stared back at him through rusting bars. The cages were connected, with an entrance from the feeding cage to the chimp loo, the primates showing enough intelligence to keep their toilet separate. As

Marvin had briefed him, Scout gave the chimps their food before closing the door to the bathroom cage. He held his breath and went through the process as quickly as possible, shovelling the mess into the pails provided.

Gonzo watched Scout's labour and pointed a crooked finger. He then slapped his leathery forehead with his dark grey hand before throwing back his head in raucous laughter—or rather shrieking—with a mouthful of large white teeth and scratching apparently itchy underarms. Scout scowled back. His back hurt, his arms ached, and he was hungry. He didn't need a stupid chimp making fun of him.

Scout put down the shovel, stuck his thumbs in his ears, and wiggled his fingers. Gonzo immediately did the same. This time Scout burst out laughing. The two engaged in a few moments of trading raspberry blowing and finger-pointing.

"I think Gonzo sees you as part of the family already," Kiki said with a chuckle.

Scout's face reddened in embarrassment. "Oh, I didn't 'ear yer."

"Of course not. A mime ain't nothing if he ain't quiet."

"Yes, I s'pose that's true," Scout said, picking his brush back up. "Yer in yer costume already?"

"I'm on duty as soon as the gates open." Kiki sat on a nearby wooden bench and regarded Scout. "Why did you join the circus anyway? Is Marvin your family?"

Scout's thin shoulders slumped. "No, well, yes. It's a bit complicated."

"Family often is, I s'pose." Kiki idly kicked at a stone.

Scout was quiet for a moment. Family was an awkward subject for him to talk about. "I was adopted a few years ago," he said finally. "I grew up on the streets of London mostly."

"An orphan, then?"

Scout picked up the broom. "Yeah,"

"But you got adopted?" Kiki raised his painted eyebrows. "I often dreamed of getting adopted. Too late for me now. Didn't your new family treat you well?"

Scout sniffed once and kept sweeping.

Kiki picked up a pebble and threw it at Scout.

Scout shot the mime a look of annoyance. "Hey!"

"Mimes talk less than most people," Kiki said, "but when we do ask a question, it's bad luck not to answer it."

Scout stuck out his tongue.

Kiki raised a gloved hand and pointed to his

painted teardrop, and Scout couldn't prevent the small smile from tugging on his lips.

"They sent me to boardin' school," Scout said.

"Oh, what a crime! A good education, right proper food, exercise, and a chance to prove yourself with good grades. That could get you into Oxford, you know. Top employers will court you if you make it through there as a lawyer or a doctor or—" Kiki threw up his hands, "I don't know what your parents are thinking!"

"It's not that, it's . . ."

Kiki stared at him expectantly.

"I don't want to talk about it, all right?"

"All right, fair enough. I don't mean to pry or anything."

"You're not pryin'," Scout said, "I'm just focused on the future, not the past."

"People who join a circus are the type who want to move on," Kiki said. "I mean literally. The human novelty acts, in particular, come from unlucky backgrounds."

Scout paused mid-sweep.

"Outcasts, really," Kiki continued.

"Yeah, outcasts," Scout agreed. Like he was. A square peg in a round hole, not fitting in at Hartigan House or with those stuck-up bullies at Kingswell.

"Watch this," Kiki said as he stood up in front of the cages with all the chimps and pantomimed taking something out of his pocket. He held the invisible object up, then peeled it like a banana. The chimps watched in rapt attention while he ate the imaginary fruit. It really looked like something was in his mouth while he chewed, his eyes nonchalantly looking around while he ate. Then he held the banana up higher and raised his eyebrows as if to offer it to the monkeys. Many gibbered away and held out their arms. Kiki then opened one of the small feeding doors and moved as if throwing the half-eaten banana into their cage. Some chimps jumped off their perches and scrambled around in the dirt, looking for the pretend treat.

Scout laughed.

Gonzo didn't. He stared at Kiki, then put his thumbs in his ears, stuck out his tongue, and blew a noisy raspberry.

Suddenly, they heard a shout of distress coming from the direction of the elephant enclosures.

Scout raced to the door. "Mr. Singh?"

More shouting had both Scout and Kiki running towards the sound. Rounding a corner, they almost ran into Mr. Quill and Mr. Rhimes. Soon, the four arrived at the main gate of the enclosure.

Inside, they found Mr. Singh kneeling on the ground near the far fence, his face in his hands. Marvin and the dog-face man were with him. All the elephants stood to one side near the opposite fence except Tulip, who stood near the centre, her ears and tail swishing violently back and forth. She bucked her head rapidly, as she had the night before in the ring.

The reason for Mr. Singh's distress was clear: Luther Bancroft, the ringmaster of Sweeney's Spectacular Circus, lay on the ground, arms and legs askew. Blood soaked the dirt around his crushed body.

"He's dead," Marvin said, looking at Scout. "Trampled by Tulip."

9

*G*inger distracted herself by going into work early at her Regent Street dress shop, Feathers & Flair. Since Rosa's birth, Ginger had been attempting to take care of her business administration from her home study, but she couldn't keep her mind on matters with Scout's current rebellious streak. A trip out and about to think about delicious fabrics and new 1927 fashion designs was what she needed.

Ginger had opened her shop shortly after she'd moved back to London at the beginning of 1924, and it had been a booming business ever since. Not that she needed money—she had plenty of that—but she needed something to do. Several years of working as a secret service agent had given her a taste of adventure and purpose. She thought indulging her love of fashion would satisfy her, but soon she'd needed more. That was when she'd opened her investigative office.

Becoming a mother had curbed her sense of need for constant challenge and excitement. Adopting Scout and having Rosa certainly qualified as challenging and exciting. At the moment, Scout was making it *too* exciting.

Ginger parked her Crossley, one tyre kissing the kerb on a side street, as she thought of Basil's words of comfort. Most certainly, after a few days of back-breaking and foul-smelling work, Scout would realise what he had as part of the Gold-Reed clan, and all this nonsense would be put behind them, never to be spoken of again.

By the time Ginger had strolled into Feathers & Flair, with Boss in her arms, the heels of her shoes tapping nicely on the polished white marble tiles, her mood had lifted.

"Good morning, everyone!"

Madame Roux, the shop's manager, lifted her head. Well into her late fifties, she kept her hair cut fashionably short, wore French designs, and walked with grace and poise that demanded respect.

Ginger lowered Boss to the floor, and he disappeared through the narrow opening of the velvet curtain—which separated the front where artificial mannequins displayed the latest Parisian fashions from the back where the fabrics were stored and the sewing was done—to where his shop bed was located.

"Mrs. Reed. How pleasant to see you." Madame Roux skirted around the sales counter and offered to take Ginger's summer coat, a black-and-cream plaid number with low front pockets, a wide collar, and matching belt. "The fabric from Paris has arrived," she said, beautifully rolling her *R*s. "I think you will be pleased with the delightful selection. They will make lovely summer gowns."

Besides Madame Roux, Ginger employed Emma, a seamstress and budding fashion designer. Dorothy helped upper-floor customers, who preferred factory designs that could be bought and worn the same day. Millie, the live mannequin, modelled original designs created for the most discerning customer. When Millie's modelling talents weren't needed, she helped Madame Roux on the floor, and in her free time, she stepped out with Constable Braxton, Basil's right-hand man.

"Good morning, Mrs. Reed, and hello, Boss!" Millie's melodious voice reached Ginger as she headed to the back, her curiosity about the new prints engaged.

"It was fabulous," Millie said, returning to her conversation with Emma. "I'd never been to a circus before. Constable Braxton insisted that I just had to go, and I'm so glad I did!"

"What fun," Emma said. "Oh, hello, Mrs. Reed."

"Were you at the circus, Mrs. Reed?" Millie asked.

"No," Ginger said, presuming her shop assistant meant opening night and not in general. "I'm not fond of such spectacles."

"It really was rather exciting. The wire walker was tantalising, and the elephants—what magnificent beasts!"

Ginger dipped her chin. "I can agree with you on that point."

"Lord and Lady Davenport-Witt were there," Millie continued. She buckled her forehead. "I could've sworn I saw your son Scout. Must have been a dup—what's that German word?"

"Doppelgänger," Ginger filled in.

Madame Roux ducked in, her French accent tinged with exasperation. "Millie, there are customers on the floor."

79

"Oh, yes." Millie shrugged apologetically. "Excuse me, madam."

One look from Madame Roux and Emma was back at her Singer sewing machine, expertly feeding smooth fabric under the little metal foot as she worked the wrought-iron pedal on the floor.

Ginger settled in the small office, feeling somewhat claustrophobic with its size and lack of windows. The electric light hanging from the ceiling was insufficient, and the bulb from the desk lamp sizzled out just as she pulled the string. *Drat!*

"Emma!" Ginger called through the adjoining door. "Do we have a spare lightbulb somewhere?"

Emma called back, "Yes. I'll get one."

Ginger returned to the back room where Dorothy was unpackaging new frocks. Dorothy held one up for her approval, a sleeveless crêpe frock in a green and rosa floral print with a ruffled trim around the neck, a pleated skirt, and a long matching scarf.

"It's lovely," Ginger said. Dorothy disappeared upstairs with an armful, and Ginger took the time to examine the new bolts of fabric. Emma dug out a lightbulb from a shelf in the corner. "I'll put it in for you, madam,"

"Thank you, Emma."

Usually, Ginger would be enthralled by the new arrivals, but this situation with Scout had scattered her thoughts.

"Are you all right, Mrs. Reed?" Madame Roux asked. "Is everything all right with the shop?"

"Yes, everything is fine." Ginger forced a smile and chastised herself for letting her emotions get in the way of her work.

"How is the beautiful baby?" Madame Roux asked. "Is she keeping you from sleeping?"

"Why? Do I look tired?" Ginger couldn't blame little Rosa for keeping her awake. For that, Scout was firmly responsible.

"No, no, *non*," Madame Roux said quickly. "You are beautiful as always."

"You are too kind, Madame Roux. And Rosa is perfect. She's with her nurse."

"I see. And the rest of your family is well, I trust?"

Ginger considered her shop manager. The lady wasn't usually so discerning, and it was very disconcerting. "We are all well, thank you. How are you, Madame Roux? Are you still dancing with Inspector Sanders?" Ginger remembered the first time she'd met the inspector. It was when a fox stole had been stolen from Feathers & Flair shortly after she'd opened Lady Gold Investigations. An unlikely friendship had been forged during the case between the jovial man, who was unpolished, and her sophisticated Parisian shop manager.

Madame Roux's painted lips tugged into an imperceptible smile. "The inspector does keep me on my toes, madame."

Ginger returned to her desk, now well lit with a new lightbulb, and went through the post, but she couldn't throw off a growing sense of unease no matter how she tried. Basil believed Scout needed to work out his discontentment, but Ginger was worried he'd be influenced in the wrong direction. Thirteen-year-old boys weren't the best at making good judgement calls.

"Emma," Ginger said as she grabbed her coat and gloves. "Do you mind looking after Boss for a while?"

The sewing machine chatter stopped as Emma looked up. "I'd be happy to, madam. Hey, Boss? You don't mind staying with me, do you?"

Boss was quite happy wherever he had a warm bed. Ginger was thankful that dogs slept a lot. It assuaged her guilt.

"Thank you, Emma. Ta-ta."

Outside, Ginger hopped into her Crossley, pulled out into traffic with a couple of welcoming horns honking, and headed south towards the circus grounds.

10

*W*hen Basil got word of the report of a body at the circus, he immediately stepped into the queue to investigate. This surprised his colleagues as the Yard rarely took an interest in a death unless it was already deemed suspicious. Basil hadn't bothered to mention his connection. He nodded at Braxton. "Come with me."

The constable secured his helmet, the chin strap resting on the base of his chin and hurried to Basil's side. "Everything all right, sir?"

"Not for some poor bloke. You'd better get down there straight away. The pathologist will be there as soon as possible, but he and his assistant are tied up with another case in East London, so it will take him a while to get there."

Basil took some comfort in the fact that the deceased was referred to as a man and not a lad, but the whole thing didn't bode well, especially since the mishap had happened near the elephants—in precisely the last spot he'd seen his son. Stepping into the passenger side of a vehicle and letting Braxton take the wheel, he said, "Get us to Clapham Common."

Thirty minutes later, Basil stood in the dusty elephant enclosure, his expression grim as he stared down at the misshapen form of ringmaster Luther Bancroft. In all his years as an investigator, he had seen nothing like this. The man had been trampled.

Constable Braxton whistled. "Awful mess, isn't it, sir?"

"Who's in charge of the elephants?" Basil asked.

An Indian man stepped forward. "I am, sir. My name is Tarjeet Singh." His heavily accented voice was steady, but his eyes were red and swollen as if he had been weeping. "I am the head animal trainer here."

"I need this area roped off," Basil instructed. "No one is to enter without my saying so."

The animal trainer had the flat look of someone in shock.

"Mr. Singh?"

"Ah, yes, sir." The man snapped his fingers, "Scout!"

Basil turned sharply at the man's use of his son's name and followed his gaze to the lad hovering in the shadows.

"You heard the chief inspector," Mr. Singh continued. "Take that rope and secure the entrance."

Scout froze as his fear-filled eyes locked with Basil's. No one in the room apart from Braxton knew of their connection. Basil gave Scout a subtle nod, and the lad ran to the tent's opening.

"Sir?" Braxton said with a tilt of his chin in Scout's direction.

"Let it be for now, Braxton."

Basil took a moment to assess the room and the occupants. Besides himself, Braxton, Singh, and Scout were Marvin, the short man he recalled went by the name of Prince, the main clown, known as Quill, the poor Ukrainian bloke who'd needed a new razor every day, and a man he'd yet to meet with oiled, jet-black hair.

The elephants were lined up in a row, back legs shackled. Basil shifted the group to the opposite end of the room from the beasts. "Who found the body?"

A pause settled on the small group before the animal trainer answered, "I did, sir."

"Can you tell me what led to that discovery?"

"I came this morning to check on the elephants, like I usually do, and . . ."

Quill broke in. "Rhimes and I heard Singh shout and came running."

Braxton chimed in. "Mr. Rhimes is an acrobat. A right good one too. He fried an omelette up there!"

Rhimes flashed a look of appreciation Braxton's way.

"Did anyone see this happen?" Basil asked.

Another pause, then Singh responded. "No. He was dead when I arrived."

"I understand that Mr. Bancroft was the ring-master," Basil started, "was it normal for him to spend time in the elephant enclosure?"

"No, sir," Mr. Singh said.

"Does anyone know why he came in?"

Another pause as the assembled men darted looks between each other. Something strange was going on, and Basil was determined to get to the bottom of it. "Any idea of what that whip is doing here?" he asked, pointing to the leather apparatus lying in the dirt.

"It's mine," Singh said, "but I never carry it into the elephant pen. I use it solely to train the tigers. It was lying there when I found Mr. Bancroft." He frowned deeply. "He must've brought it in with vengeful intentions."

Basil stepped towards the line of elephants and then stopped. He had never been this close to such fearsome beasts before and wasn't eager to get closer. As docile as they seemed right now, one apparently had violence in its heart. The creatures' legs were as big as tree stumps. The largest one on the end had what appeared to be blood on its feet.

Basil pointed. "Would that one be the culprit?"

Singh sighed, giving a slight nod. "That's Tulip."

"Careful," Braxton commented. "That thing looks like it could crush a tank."

Singh shot Braxton a withering look. "I assure you, Tulip is kinder than most humans."

"I bet Bancroft came to taunt her," Marvin said. "She humiliated him during the show."

"How so?" Basil asked.

Braxton chuckled but immediately quieted at Basil's glare.

"Mind sharing what's so funny, Constable?"

"Nothing, sir, just me and Millie were at the show. That elephant knocked off the ringmaster's hat then knocked him to the ground with her trunk. The whole crowd roared with laughter. I thought it was part of the show."

Quill, the King of Clowns, snorted. "Bancroft didn't have a humorous bone in his body."

Rhimes, with arms folded over his chest, agreed. "He certainly didn't like to be laughed at."

"So, you think he came to teach the elephant a lesson?"

All eyes turned to the feminine voice, and Basil's lips twitched at the sight of Ginger, standing on the other side of the rope.

Basil tipped his hat to her, then to Scout, said, "Let your mother in."

"Mother?" Prince said. He elbowed Petrenko in the thigh. "If I had a mother like that, I wouldn't run away to join a dumpy circus."

Basil scowled at the man, effectively quieting him.

"This is my wife, Mrs. Reed," Basil said. "She's also known in London as Lady Gold of Lady Gold Investigations and often consults with the Metropolitan Police."

Ginger, who prided herself in keeping up with the fashion trends, looked very much out of place with this grubby lot. She wore an emerald green day frock with embroidered triangular pockets, a matching belt, and matching triangular accents on the long sleeves. The wide collar featured a dainty, low-hanging black, knotted scarf. She held out a gloved hand to Singh. "I don't believe we've met."

"I'm Singh," the animal trainer said. "It's a pleasure."

"Now, did I hear you say you didn't bring that whip here?"

Singh bowed slightly. "That's right, madam."

"Curious." Ginger pushed a strand of red hair behind her ear, causing the dangling jewelled earring to swing. "Scout, which animal is the one in question?"

Scout stepped towards the elephants and pointed. "Tulip, at the end. She's as gentle as a lamb. She wouldn't have hurt anyone. Not on purpose."

Basil shared a look with Ginger, both of them noticing the return of the *H*s in Scout's speech.

"It wouldn't have been the first time Mr. Bancroft had stolen into Tulip's pen and taken a whip to her," Mr. Quill said.

"Why would he do such a thing?" Basil asked.

"Cuz he's a vicious blighter," Prince said.

"So, what then?" Basil said. "He came in here sometime after—"

"It would have been in the middle of the night," Mr. Singh offered.

"All right, in the middle of the night," Basil said. "Then he took the whip to the elephant—"

"Tulip," Scout said, interrupting.

"Righto, Tulip," Basil said. "She rears up, and Bancroft loses his footing, getting in her way when she comes down again."

Ginger, in her heeled shoes, carefully walked across the dusty floor. "This is where Mr. Bancroft was found?"

Singh nodded. "Yes, madam."

"And the elephants are over there," Ginger stated.

Basil followed her gaze. "There aren't any drag marks."

"No," Ginger said. "Mr. Bancroft didn't try to get away."

"The elephant must've come to him," Basil returned. He turned to Singh. "Your elephant couldn't have reached Mr. Bancroft while being manacled to that post." Basil pointed to the iron manacle attached to Tulip's left rear foot and then looked over at a very sturdy-looking wooden post pounded into the ground. There was a thick chain leading from the post to the manacle.

Singh sighed again. "That is correct."

"And no blood anywhere around where the

elephant, Tulip, is now standing." He turned to look at the animal trainer whose olive-coloured skin had paled.

"Dear God, man," Rhimes spouted. "Did you forget to chain her up last night?"

"I did not!" Singh shook his head vehemently. "I would never do such a stupid thing. I check the animals' chains every night and the doors to all cages. I swear to you, she was chained last night. I found her unchained this morning, and deeply distressed. I managed to calm her and re-secure the shackle."

"Then how can this be explained?" Basil asked.

"For these manacles, there are two sets of keys." Singh produced one from his pocket. "This one, which I always keep on my person. The other one is kept in that box over there." Singh pointed to a metal key safe hanging on one of the posts holding up the roof that partially covered the enclosure. The padlock on the box was open as was the cover to the box. Inside were several key hooks. Singh stepped up to it, giving it a closer look.

"The key is hanging from the wrong hook," he said soberly. "Someone broke into that box, stole the key, and unlocked the manacle."

"Are you suggesting he was murdered?" Quill asked incredulously.

A soft voice responded, "Many of you wanted him dead. It was only a matter of opportunity."

Kiki stood on the other side of the rope, his face white with black tears and an oversized frown making him look like he was in mourning. Everyone stared back, slack-jawed, glaring at the mime's audacity.

"I'm right, aren't I?" the lad said with a hint of jest. "Just last night, one of you announced that he would kill Mr. Bancroft."

Basil's blood cooled as everyone shifted to look at his son.

"Scout?" he said.

"It was me, Dad," Scout said, his voice breaking. "But I didn't do it, I swear."

11

A hole had opened up in the elephant enclosure, and Scout was about to fall in. Stars clouded his vision, and his knees melted. He gulped as everyone in the room stared at him with suspicion, horror, and disbelief.

"Scout?" his dad said softly. Mum stepped to his side. He'd always been short but had grown recently, tall enough that his mother needn't kneel to look him in the eyes anymore. His humiliation was bad enough without adding to it!

"It's all right," she said. Lowering her voice further, she added, "Your father and I know you would never do something like this. We'll take care of it."

"We all heard him," Mr. Rhimes said sombrely,

breaking the quiet. "He said he would kill him, clear as day."

"He'd been on the grog," Prince added. "He didn't know what he was doing."

Scout appreciated the dwarf trying to come to his defence, though it was a bit backwards.

Mum looked down at Scout with a frown. "The grog?"

"I only had one sip," Scout said. "I didn't even like it. Everyone else was drinking too."

"Yeah, if being drunk makes a murderer," Marvin punched his palm with his fist, "then everyone 'ere could be guilty."

"Poppycock," Mr. Quill said. "The booze is beside the point. The lad was the only one to threaten Bancroft's life."

"He's a boy of thirteen," Ginger protested. "Hardly capable of taking on a full-grown man like Mr. Bancroft."

Scout felt a bit slighted and embarrassed at his mum coming to his defence like that. He wasn't a child anymore!

"It doesn't take brute strength to unlock a shackle," Mr. Rhimes said. "It might not be the brightest act, but any spiteful person could do it, no matter their size."

"Don't forget that he pretended to be one of us," Mr. Quill said. "Yet here are his posh parents. The rascal knows he can get away with anything."

With his rich accented voice, Mr. Petrenko said, "Even murder."

The small group got so loud that they upset the elephants. Poor Tulip. None of this was her fault. Scout slipped away from his accusers—some family they'd turned out to be!—and approached Tulip. Her round brown eyes seemed to express the regret they shared. None of this was her fault—or his! Carefully, he lifted his arm. Tulip gently wrapped her trunk around it, letting out a grunt of affection.

"It's going to be all right, old girl," Scout whispered.

"Scout!"

Scout turned to his mother's worried voice. "It's fine, Mum," he said. "Tulip wouldn't hurt a flea."

"And yet a man is dead."

Scout swivelled toward Kiki's voice, the mime still standing on the other side of the rope.

"Kiki?" Scout said, approaching. "I thought we were friends."

"No such thing as friends in the circus," Kiki said, his face drawn in what looked like real sorrow.

"Only survival. You seem like a nice enough lad. I've got nothing against you, personally."

Scout's dad clapped his hands, demanding attention. "See here. None of us know what happened here, but I promise you I will get to the bottom of it." Turning to Mr. Singh, he continued, "I want you to help Constable Braxton draw up a list of people who would have known about the history between the elephant called Tulip and Mr. Bancroft." His gaze then slowly swept across everyone standing there. "No one is to leave here before being questioned by either me or Constable Braxton."

At his mother's urging, Scout left Tulip and came to her side. When his father joined them, his mum said, "I want to send Scout home."

"I promise I'll behave," Scout said. There was no place he'd rather be in this moment and time than in his warm bed, eating Mrs. Beasley's shortbread biscuits and snuggling with Boss.

His dad seemed to consider Scout gravely, and Scout was pretty sure he could read his mind. Despite his parents' protestations, he was a suspect. The *prime* suspect.

After a long breath, his dad said the words Scout wanted to hear. "That can be arranged."

. . .

Ginger hadn't expected to walk in on a crime scene, and she definitely hadn't expected her son to be suspected of murder.

"Basil?" she said with an imploring lilt in her voice. "I believe you're in conflict."

Basil let out a quick, sharp breath. He knew, as did Ginger, that if he didn't volunteer to step down, Superintendent Morris would force his hand.

"Braxton," Basil said, calling his constable over. "Contact the Yard. Have them send over another inspector to head up this investigation."

Constable Braxton tipped his chin, his helmet slipping forward slightly. "Yes, sir."

Ginger tapped Basil's arm. "Perhaps *you* could take Scout home."

Basil gave her a look. "And what do you plan to do, then?"

"I think I'll hang around here."

As a private citizen, Ginger didn't have the restrictions that her husband had regarding police protocol. Her experience as a private investigator came in handy in situations like this. She and Basil had an understanding. She would be his eyes and ears.

"Very well," Basil said, then leaning in so Ginger alone could hear him. "Be careful. It's likely that one of this lot is a murderer and might kill again."

"I shall watch my step and my back," Ginger said as reassuringly as possible.

Constable Braxton returned with shortened breath, indicating he'd been running. "Vance is reporting back to the Yard, sir."

"Stay with Mrs. Reed," Basil said. "At least until the new inspector arrives."

Ginger laid a hand on Scout's shoulder. "It's time for you to go home, son."

Scout, duly chastised by the tragedy and still wearing his embarrassment at getting called out, ducked his head and joined Basil as he headed for the exit. "Bye, Mum," he said, adding with a mumble. "I'm sorry."

"Things will work out," Ginger said. "Now, go home and cheer up Boss." It was understood that Dorothy would see that the dog got safely back to Hartigan House should Ginger need to leave him behind at Feathers & Flair for any reason.

Basil glanced back at her over his shoulder with a look of uncertainty.

"I'll be fine," Ginger said. "I'm with these fine constables." She patted her small handbag. "Remi is with me."

Remi, meaning her Remington pistol.

Looking on at this exchange were the men Basil had gathered together in the elephant enclosure. They stood as far away from the large animals as possible. Tulip was back in her shackles, thanks to the efficient work of Mr. Singh. Grouped with the animal trainer was the dwarf, the man with hypertrichosis, the King of Clowns, the mime, the wire walker, and Marvin.

"Is it really necessary to keep us here?" Mr. Quill rubbed the back of his neck. "I've got things to do before tonight's show."

"'Ow are we doing a show?" Marvin asked. "Who will act as ringmaster?"

"I can do it," Mr. Rhimes said.

"You'll be busy defying gravity," Mr. Quill countered. "I can do it. The show must go on."

"Only if every interview is finished," Braxton said sternly.

Mr. Petrenko nervously stroked his face. "Are you saying we all are suspects?"

"At the moment," Ginger said.

"Ha, that's rich!" Mr. Quill scratched his head. "Your lad sets an elephant free, and we're to blame? Of course, of course. How could a lad of your ilk be guilty?"

"What was he doin' here, anyway?" Mr. Rhimes asked. His eyes scanned Ginger from her crystal hat pin to her leather T-strap shoes, as if he were taking in her Regent Street fashion.

"'E ran away," Marvin said. "Silly idiot. Tossing his good fortune away like that."

Ginger held Marvin's gaze. He was one to talk. She'd pulled strings to keep him out of jail by getting him a position in the navy, and he'd used his fists to jeopardise good employment serving king and country, ending up working at a circus?

As if reading her mind, Marvin shrugged. "I don't judge the lad, though. A man 'as to find 'is own way."

"And look where it got him," Mr. Quill said. "Blood on his hands."

"Mr. Quill," Ginger said sharply. "In England, the law still states a person is innocent until proven guilty."

Mr. Quill snorted, then sat on an overturned bucket. Everyone stared at Ginger and the waiting constables with a narrow look of contempt. Appropriately, the mime was the only one to stay silent, neither accusing nor defending himself.

Constable Braxton had a notepad and pencil out.

"In the meantime, I'll take down all your particulars. Legal name, address, and the like."

Ginger looked around. Dust floated in the air, which smelled of animals kept in captivity, dirty and nervous. The elephants proved to be a little unsettled, watching the people in the room with round brown eyes, shifting heavily from flat foot to flat foot. The younger ones had lost interest and lay on the hay near their mothers, one snoring adorably, his mouth open and little trunk wrapped around his mother's leg.

Carefully, Ginger approached the matriarch, staying just out of reach. "Hi, Tulip," she said softly. "What happened here?"

Tulip raised her trunk, let out a quiet bellow, and turned her head to better catch Ginger's eye better. If elephants could talk, Ginger was certain Tulip would tell her everything.

Tulip extended her trunk as if in greeting. Ginger slowly reached out her hand, allowing the animal to sniff it, her trunk gently stroking Ginger's palm.

"You didn't mean to do it, did you?" Ginger said. In the depth of her heart, she believed the majestic beast had been provoked. Ginger was determined to prove her son's innocence, but she also needed to prove Tulip's before an edict for her termination was handed down.

The police arrived, a small contingent amounting to two officers and an inspector.

"Hello, Inspector Sanders," Ginger said.

"Mrs. Reed! Good t' see you again, but I 'ave to admit, I wish it were under better circumstances." The jolly inspector had bright, blue eyes, a substantial grey moustache, and a paunchy stomach.

"As do I."

"Madame Roux don't like me comin' into the shop. Not sophisticated enough, she says."

"Oh, Inspector—"

"I don't mind. She's quite right. I'm lucky a lady like 'er will see me. Even if it's only under cover of darkness!" He laughed at his joke, then turned, immediately sobered by the sight of the body on the ground. He waved Constable Braxton to his side. "Give me the details, Constable."

By the time Constable Braxton had finished his verbal report, Dr. Gupta, the pathologist, had arrived. The Indian-born doctor and Ginger had crossed paths on several occasions and were friendly, if not strictly friends.

"Good day, Dr. Gupta," Ginger said.

"Good day, Mrs. Reed, Inspector Sanders," the pathologist returned. "What have we here?"

"A body was found just after dawn," Ginger said, leading the way to Bancroft's corpse. "He appears to have been trampled."

After a cursory examination of the body, Dr. Gupta said, "I can confirm that the apparent cause of death was a crushing blow by a heavy weight. There's also a strong scent of whisky on his person."

Ginger had picked up the odour as well. That could have explained Mr. Bancroft's poor judgement in the elephant pen.

"'Ow long has he been deceased?" Inspector Sanders asked.

"The body's in full rigor." Dr. Gupta studied the face of his wristwatch. "I'd approximate the man came to his demise between midnight and two in the morning."

The doctor left when the ambulance attendants removed the body to take it to the mortuary.

Inspector Sanders asked for a place to set up interviews, and a small tent was cleared out for his use. He paused at the door, causing Ginger to come to a stop. "Can't really let you come inside now, Mrs. Reed. Official police business and all that you know."

"But . . ."

"I know you and the chief inspector have an understandin' and the super, for reasons many of us underlin's don't understand, chooses to turn a blind eye." He cupped his mouth and lowered his voice. "But I know you, and your reputation, madam, so, I'll just leave the door open like this, see? What you do in the corridor 'ere, is none of my business."

Ginger tilted her head. "Thank you, Inspector."

Inspector Sanders stepped inside, and with a loud voice said, "I'd like to see the King o' Clowns, Mr. Quill."

12

*G*inger pretended to be bothered by a loose thread in her scarf as Constable Braxton led a disgruntled Mr. Quill through the door flaps of the tent. Another officer, standing near the door, nodded politely and turned away. Despite the discretion of the officers who respected Basil and, by extension, Ginger herself, she still found it difficult to see through the flap that, unaided by a breeze that would most certainly be welcomed, lay shut. Ginger could not see inside, and the conversation between Inspector Sanders and Mr. Quill was muffled.

Eyeing the canvas of the temporary dwelling, Ginger noted that the fabric was well worn, thinning in spots to the point of creating small holes, perhaps the work of moths. Ginger inconspicuously stepped away from the officer waiting outside and circled the tent until she found what she was looking for—a peep hole.

Through the small opening, she could see two foldable wooden chairs, one occupied by Inspector Sanders, his trousers hoisted up to reveal a pair of mismatched patterned socks, and the other by Mr. Quill. The King of Clowns' ruddy face, now without make-up, was pulled into a deep frown as he ran a hand through greasy hair.

Ginger wondered why Inspector Sanders had called on the clown instead of the animal trainer, the most likely suspect. But perhaps that was why—the inspector was gathering testimony in the order of the least likely culprit to the most.

"I tell you," he said, "Bancroft was alive when I last saw him." Mr. Quill snorted through large nostrils. "And he was furious. I've seen the man angry plenty of times. It didn't take much to set the bloke off, but public humiliation—well, that's something he couldn't tolerate."

"Tell me what 'appened when the circus ended," Inspector Sanders said. "After the audience went 'ome."

"Same stuff as usual. The props were put away

for safekeeping, the animals were secured in their cages and stalls, and the performers got out of costume. Those who work here sometimes gather for something to eat or drink. Most keep to themselves."

"And the group that met together with you?" Inspector Sanders asked.

"We are heads of the departments, so we socialise occasionally."

"You're the 'ead of the clown group," Inspector Sanders started, "and Mr. Singh oversees the animals. What about the others 'oo were with you?"

"Rhimes runs the acrobats, and Petrenko heads up the novelty acts," Mr. Quill replied. "The dwarf is his sidekick. You see one; you usually find the other."

Inspector Sanders made a show of reviewing his notepad. "And the others? Marvin Elliot, Scout Elliot, I mean Reed, and the mime, Kiki?"

"Newcomers. The two lads have recently been taken on by Singh, and the mime is new to me. I don't handled the hiring." With a shrug, Mr. Quill continued his explanation. "The business is too transient for my time and trouble. We often let the new ones hang around us until they get their footing. The circus is very transient, Inspector, and confusing for new people." Cupping his chin, he added, "Besides, the mime intrigues me."

Inspector Sanders' round head popped up, his bushy eyebrows rising with interest. "Oh? 'Owso?"

Mr. Quill leaned forward and placed a hand on his lower back, groaning as if it ached. "I dunno. He plays his part well. I appreciate a good act."

"What's goin' to 'appen now?" Inspector Sanders asked. "With the circus?"

With a creepy sad-face smile, the King of Clowns said, "Someone else will have to take Bancroft's place."

"And 'oo would that be?"

"Probably me, Inspector."

Ginger shifted her weight and switched to her other eye. In doing so, she accidentally leaned in to the canvas of the tent.

"What's that?" Mr. Quill said.

Inspector Sanders narrowed his eyes, looking in Ginger's direction. She pulled back. "Just the wind, I s'pose," the inspector said, covering for her. "Now, explain why you would be the next choice for ringmaster?"

Quill shrugged, a smug grin forming on his face. "Seniority, sir."

. . .

Marvin was next to be called into the tent. Ginger found she held her breath. Not that she thought Marvin could be guilty of murder, but he could certainly be framed, and whoever pulled off this murder was cunning indeed.

"Mr. Elliot." Inspector Sanders stroked his moustache as he began. "Tell me what you knew about Mr. Bancroft before he passed away?"

Marvin shifted nervously in his chair. Ginger knew her son's cousin didn't like the law and had been guilty of misdemeanours in the past. His discomfiture had a way of making him look suspicious.

"Not much, sir," Marvin said. "'Ardly knew the fella."

"'E didn't take you on?" Inspector Sanders asked.

"No, sir. That would be Mr. Singh."

"You were at the small gathering after opening night, along with your cousin?"

Marvin nodded. "Uh-huh."

"So, you 'eard him threaten Mr. Bancroft?"

"Well, 'ey . . . wait a minute. Scout ain't a killer. 'E's just a bit spirited, 'e is. It was just in jest."

"'As Scout ever threatened anyone else?" Inspector Sanders leaned in. "In jest?"

Ginger's heart skipped a beat as she waited for Marvin's answer.

"Not in my 'earin', no."

"'Ow long 'ave you been working for the circus, Mr. Elliot?"

Marvin worked his lips. "I dunno. Ten days. Eleven?"

"You 'ave a lot of affection for your cousin, don't you?"

"Yeah. 'E's a great lad."

"You'd do anything for him?"

Ginger had the uneasy sense Inspector Sanders was setting the boy up.

Marvin narrowed his gaze. "Yeah . . ."

"Even kill for him?"

"No. Not that. Especially not over some dumb animal."

"Where were you between one and two this morning?"

Marvin hesitated, then answered. "In me bed, sir. Ask Singh."

Inspector Sanders worked his lips. Being asleep in one's bed at that time of night wasn't unusual and a frustrating fact for any investigating officer. Especially when one suspect can provide a loose alibi for another. The inspector said, "Thank you, Mr. Elliot." To Constable Braxton, he called out, "Send in Mr. Petrenko."

Ginger stretched out as she waited, holding on to her cloche hat. She'd been standing in the dirt for some time now and frowned at the dust on her shiny black T-strap shoes. Peeking through the eye hole dried out her eyes, and she blinked them. Inspector Sanders was staring her way when she looked through the hole again.

"Would you like a chair, Mrs. Reed?"

Before she could answer, Constable Braxton returned with Mr. Petrenko. Though she would appreciate sitting, she wouldn't be able to reach the peephole that way.

"Mr. Petrenko, I understand you're the 'ead of the novelty acts."

"Yes, sir," he replied with his Slavic accented voice. "I am."

"And what is your role, exactly?"

Mr. Petrenko stroked the hair on his face. "As you see, I am spectacle. My role is to let people stare and laugh."

Ginger felt a morsel of pity. Life was indeed unfair, and it had to be nearly intolerable for some. It wasn't poor judgement or fate that kept people like

Mr. Petrenko from living normal, happy lives, but chance. Rare birth defects gave people like this very few choices in life, especially when it came to survival.

"'Ow long 'ave you worked for this circus, Mr. Petrenko?"

"Since it started, sir. A scout recruited me into employ of Mr. Bancroft."

"What did you think of that?"

"He offered work for people like me, sir. It is help we need and did not get from government or our families. My family had recently come to live in England." Sadness flashed behind blue eyes. "They were happy to rid themselves of me."

"I see. Did you like Mr. Bancroft?"

"The man was bully, sir. Did not have thread of kindness or consideration in him. He refused to pay Prince properly, demeaning him by paying him child wages." After blowing a breath of frustration, he continued, "But he gave me bed and food for my belly. I did my best to stay out of his way."

"Do you know of anyone who'd want Mr. Bancroft dead?" Inspector Sanders asked.

Mr. Petrenko let out a bark-like laugh. "You mean who would *most* like Bancroft dead?"

"If you prefer."

After another habitual stroke of his face, Mr. Petrenko leaned in. "Rhimes and Bancroft have bad blood that goes long way back. If I were betting man, I would put my money on Rhimes."

13

When Inspector Sanders asked to be directed to the loo, Ginger decided she could also use a good stretch of her legs. Unfortunately, she miscalculated the position of the next tent peg and the corresponding rope. Her toe caught, and she ungracefully fell to her knees. Her mind first registered gratitude that she was without an audience, and then she felt regret at the damage to her stockings.

Something reached for her, gripping her shoulder. Instantly she grabbed the object—a hand—and in a well-practised move, she flipped the offender onto his back on the ground as she sprang back to her feet, her hands in fists as she stood defensively.

"I warn you," she said, "I have a pistol."

A low groan in a man's voice reached her. "It's me, madam."

Ginger's eyes, growing accustomed to the darkened area, squinted at the small form, a man with short legs and arms.

"Prince Natukunda?"

The man pushed himself into a seated position. "I apologise, madam. I didn't mean to startle you."

"I'm sorry for what I did to you," Ginger said. She would have offered a hand but didn't want to offend the man, knowing he was quite capable of getting to his feet on his own. He did so, patting the dust off his trousers.

Ginger used the moment to examine her outfit. Thank goodness, her frock was intact, though as she'd expected, a ladder ran down her shin from the newly formed hole in the knee of her stocking.

"Well, we're both uninjured," Ginger said. "That's the main thing. Now, Prince Natukunda, what were you doing, prowling around the interrogation tent?"

Prince Natukunda stared up. "I suppose I could ask the same thing of you, madam."

"I imagine we were doing the same thing, from different sides of the tent." Ginger pursed her lips and cocked her head with a hint of defiance. "Were you concerned about your friend Mr. Petrenko?"

"Certainly, but not because I think he killed Bancroft. I know he didn't. He was with me."

"You share sleeping quarters?" Ginger asked.

"Indeed, we do."

"So, you're each other's alibi."

"I suppose you could say that."

Mr. Bancroft was known for his cruelty, and Ginger didn't doubt this man, Prince Natukunda, and all the novelty acts had, at one time, been the object of Mr. Bancroft's ridicule. But had the ringmaster driven one of them to murder?

Ginger lifted her chin, asking, "Do you know who did it?"

"What if I said it was Scout?" the prince returned. "Would you believe me?"

"No, I would not."

"Then forgive me, but perhaps you shouldn't be asking the questions."

Ginger blinked at the little man's audacity, but the man quickly backtracked.

"Forgive me, madam, I'm just a little shaken up, as we all are."

"That's understandable," Ginger said. "Do you

mind if I ask, how long had you known Mr. Bancroft?"

"Many years, madam. I was discovered when I was a lad of eight, discarded on the street by my own ma." He waved a short arm. "For men like me, it is best if I stay with a group. The circus is my home, and everyone is my family. Except for—"

"Scout?" Ginger ventured. Scout was new and wouldn't be counted as family by the prince.

"And that Kiki fellow." His expression twisted as if the thought of the mime was unpleasant.

"You don't like Kiki?" Ginger asked.

"Not particularly. He's not been around that long, only a day or so, but he's always in costume. I don't trust a man who refuses to show his face. But it's not the clowns I would be questioning."

Ginger raised a thinly plucked brow. "Oh? Who then?"

"I'm not one for gossip, madam, but . . ." He stepped closer and lowered his voice. "Rhimes has problems with anger. He had a row with Bancroft and threatened to leave and move to America. Bancroft laughed in his face and called him a coward. He said Rhimes didn't have the guts. Rhimes took a swing, but Bancroft ducked it in time."

"That's a remarkable story," Ginger said. "Did anyone else witness this?"

"No. And neither man was aware of my presence."

"Prince Natukunda," Ginger started, "I hope you don't find me too forward, but you're not really a prince from Africa, are you?"

The little man snickered. "I let my guard down with you, eh? I'm an Englishman through and through, and once I open my mouth, I can't hide it. My name is boring—Billy Smith. Bancroft thought the prince story would be more exciting for folks. Now, if you will forgive me, madam, I have things I must attend to."

"Certainly," Ginger said. "I wish you a good night."

"Thank you, madam." After a bow, the little man disappeared between the tents, more adept, apparently, at dodging the tent pegs and ropes than Ginger was.

Ginger found her way to the front of the tent. The officer who'd been standing there was gone, as was Constable Braxton. Where had everyone gone? Looking for a friendly face, she finally found one.

"Marvin!"

"Lady Gold," Marvin returned. "Is everything all right?"

"Yes, everything is fine. I'm looking for Inspector Sanders."

"'E and 'is men are in the stands, madam. Waitin' for the show to begin."

Inspector Sanders and his officers would keep an eye on everyone by acting like spectators. Ginger assumed he'd continue his interviews in the morning.

"Are you all right, Marvin?" Ginger noticed the skin around the lad's right eye had a pink hue, though it could have just been a trick of poor lighting.

"I'm fine, madam. Sorry for Scout being dragged over the coals like that, but 'e's with you. 'E'll be fine."

Marvin excused himself and hurried off. Ginger hoped he was right about Scout coming out of this experience unscathed, but she worried about Marvin. She'd thought about offering him work at Hartigan House, but that would pit him against Scout, making them servant and master, and that was something she was reluctant to do. Marvin was a man now, and she'd have to trust he'd make his way.

14

*B*asil sat at his desk at police headquarters at Scotland Yard, deep in thought. The whole business with Scout troubled him greatly, and it was hard to concentrate on the paperwork that he was meant to spend his day completing.

He was confident that Sanders would get to the bottom of things, and no doubt Ginger would make sure no stone was unturned. Furthermore, he was convinced of Scout's innocence. Of course he was. The lad *had been* rather rough around the edges when Ginger had taken him in three years earlier, but he never had, not once, shown any propensity for violence or even ill will towards any living thing, beast or human. It was outlandish that he would have stolen that key in some devious plan to have someone trampled to death.

But still, it was no small thing to have your thirteen-year-old son a prime suspect in a terrible murder.

Blast it! Basil fidgeted at his desk, unable to focus. What he needed was fieldwork, a distraction, something other than pushing a pencil about. There must be something else, a new case the roster.

"This is the second time you've asked to jump the queue in a week, Reed." Superintendent Morris eyed Basil suspiciously when he asked to be assigned, the superior's thick torso heaving as if he'd just walked the path around the Serpentine rather than simply hoisting himself to his feet.

"I'm sorry, sir," said Basil. "I'm just feeling the need to get away from the desk."

"Very well. There's been a complaint of bare-knuckle fighting." Morris hollered at one of the officers manning reception. "Get the address for that complaint."

Basil knew such fight clubs existed. Usually, they were held in some obscure warehouse down by the docks. Crowds of men gathered to watch pugilists beat each other senseless while gambling bets were made. Each event comprised several matches.

Contestants fought for notoriety and the sometimes-considerable purses collected from the onlookers.

Naturally, polite society frowned upon the fights, although there were no formal regulations banning them. The gambling part was technically illegal, but even this was generally regarded as unenforceable.

"What is the directive?" Basil asked.

"Several known extortionists have become involved in fixing these matches," Morris said. "Fighters are being paid to lose fights, and this, in turn, is causing some rather nasty disputes. When it starts to clog up our court systems, we have to look into it."

A while later, Basil, uncharacteristically dressed in dungarees, flat cap, and leather working boots—he kept the costume in the bottom drawer of his filing cabinet—walked into the ground floor of a five-storey shipping warehouse in the busy shipping district of Wapping. A cigarette hung from his mouth as he approached a man in overalls shouting instructions to underlings. Basil's attire accomplished the intended purpose as the burly man barely glanced at him when asked if there was a fight on.

Glancing up from his clipboard, he pointed his chin to large double doors at the back of the warehouse. "First floor," he said gruffly.

Oddly enough, the warehouse, which Basil guessed would normally bustle with activity now, was empty of personnel. On the floor were stacks of crates and boxes with labels such as sugar, dried goods, and spices, sitting in disarray on the rough wooden floor, waiting to be organised and stacked.

Basil climbed the wide wrought-iron steps up to the first floor, following the sound of men shouting. He entered a large high-ceilinged storage area where about fifty men were gathered in a circle. He could just make out the heads and shoulders of two bare-chested men in the middle, hiding their bloody faces behind bare fists.

As Basil approached, a roar went up as a bald man in his early thirties fell backwards, hitting the floor. The other fighter, a brawny, tow-headed man of about the same age, exultantly raised both hands. The left side of his face was puffy and bruised. A bloody grin revealed a missing tooth.

Pandemonium ensued as the circle was filled with men shaking the fighter's hand and slapping his back in approval, while others turned dejectedly away.

"What the deuce?" Basil said aloud as his eyes fell on the familiar face of Marvin Elliot. On the other side of the room, wearing a dirty white shirt and a towel around his neck, the lad stood, his hair tousled and one eye blackened. He'd been fighting!

As Basil approached, Marvin's eyes moved from confusion to recognition, his mouth falling open. "Sir? What are you doing 'ere?"

"I could ask you the same thing."

"I, er—"

"Did you win?"

Marvin hesitated. Would he tell the truth or spin a tale? Basil shot a pointed look at Marvin's cut-up knuckles.

"I did," he said, apparently deciding a lie would be useless. He defiantly added, "Won more money than I'd make in two months at the circus."

"Let's talk." Basil pointed his chin towards a bench sitting against a far wall a good distance from the rest of the men.

"I already gave my statement to your man," Marvin said as they turned to walk to the bench. "You said we was free to leave after we was interviewed. I 'ope you dinnt come all this way to arrest me."

"No, I didn't," Basil said as they sat down.

Marvin held his side as he slowly bent down to sit.

"Ribs?" Basil asked.

"Yeah, but I 'urt 'im worse, I'll wager."

"When did you start fighting?" Basil asked.

"In the navy. Boxing, it was, with gloves and rules. I 'ad a knack for it right off. No money for me there, though."

Basil wondered how much to probe him about this. He wasn't his father, and a lecture about safety and setting a good example wouldn't be received well by a young man like Marvin.

Marvin rubbed the back of his head. "So, what're yer 'ere for, then?"

"Police business."

"That's why you're dressed like that?"

"That's right."

"Yer closin' the fight club?"

"If I find something illegal."

"I was 'ere when Bancroft was killed," Marvin said. "I dinnt tell your man that, but now yer know. Lots of blokes saw me. I got an alibi." He slowly rose to his feet. "And Scout didn't do it, neither."

"I know," Basil said, joining him. "Are you going back to the circus now?"

"It's a place to sleep," Marvin said. He held Basil's gaze. "Just so yer know, I'm really glad Scout is wiv you and the missus."

"I am too," Basil said.

Marvin offered a nod before turning to leave.

"Elliot?" Basil called out.

Marvin slowed and looked over his shoulder.

Basil lifted his chin. "Do take care."

"I will, sir," Marvin said with a pained smile. "I will."

15

The next day, Ginger took a deep breath as she gently tapped on the closed door leading to Scout's bedroom. He'd not come out since arriving home from the circus, refusing to come down for breakfast or to talk. Ginger had never had any trouble with the little boy Scout she'd met on the SS *Rosa* and taken into her care even as she took him into her heart. That young Scout had had an indelible toothy grin and a determined spirit that could take on giants. This older, moodier Scout was an enigma to Ginger and put her in a position she rarely experienced. That of not being sure of what to do.

"Scout," she said softly. "Can I come in?"

An indecipherable muffle reached her, and Ginger accepted that it meant the affirmative.

Scout was curled up on the bed, which seemed smaller now that he had grown, though his eyes flashed with the struggle one felt when trekking through those years that took one from child to man —a foot in each world and neither leg firmly planted.

She smiled when she spotted Boss, tucked in close to Scout's torso, Scout's arm draped over Boss' neck. It seemed the dog knew what Scout needed now—time and rest.

Ginger sat at the bottom of the bed and clasped her fingers together. "I want you to know that we're not angry with you. We're just very concerned."

Scout sniffed, and he appeared to want to say something, but the trembling of his lips, tight around his teeth, caused him to look away instead.

"We're relieved that you're home, and I promise we'll work things out over time."

"I don't want to go back," Scout choked out, his voice cracking.

"To the circus?" Ginger asked incredulously, as if that was even a possibility.

"To school. I hate it there. I don't fit in. I'll never be like those lads."

"All right," Ginger said. She didn't know what they'd do instead, but there were other options. Perhaps she'd see if his tutor, Mr. Fulton, would return, or there could be other, more suitable schools. Kingswell Academy had been a default school due to its nearness, and many of Ginger and Basil's peers sent their children there. Basil himself was an alumnus.

"What do you want to do?" Ginger said, then qualified. "Just as a starting point. Ultimately, we'll have to decide your next steps together."

Scout appeared to cheer a little, even with the compromise. "I want to be a jockey, Mum. I want to learn about horses."

This wasn't news to Ginger. Ever since she'd brought Goldmine home, Scout had been enthralled, and he showed a natural aptitude when it came to understanding the nature and spirit of horses and was a natural in the saddle. His naturally diminutive size was perfectly fitted for the sport.

It would be an unorthodox choice for the offspring of someone of their family's social status, but wasn't that exactly what Basil had done when he'd stayed with Scotland Yard after the war?

"You know, I think there's a special school where you get an education whilst studying the equine industry," Ginger said. "I'll investigate it. In the meantime, I'd like you to have a bath and dress for the day. Be ready to join us for dinner later."

Scout pushed himself up into a sitting position, his eyes glistening. "Yes, Mum," he said. He had a handkerchief at the ready and wiped his eyes and nose. Ginger suppressed the urge to congratulate him on not using the sleeve of his shirt! Scout had made more progress in his evolution from street urchin to respected son of the peerage than he realised.

"Good." Ginger patted Scout's leg, then took a little more time to scrub Boss' black ears.

"We'll see both of you a little later."

After leaving Scout, and feeling much encouraged, Ginger popped into the nursery to see Rosa. Ginger's pride for her little daughter, who by rights had done nothing but exist to actually deserve the sentiment, was tremendous, and she gave Rosa a kiss on her cherub cheeks to emphasise it. Motherhood was extremely good when it was good, and as she thought about Scout, extremely hard when it was hard.

Lizzie popped into the nursery, curtsied, and said, "Excuse me, madam, but Mrs. Beasley would like to know if you wanted to approve tomorrow's menu."

Ginger's mind immediately went to the catalogue of choices, knowing Mrs. Beasley was an expert in her field, with roasts and meat pies her speciality.

Ginger shifted Rosa to her other arm. She honestly didn't even know for certain when she and Basil would be home. It all depended on how the case was going by then.

"Did she have a suggestion?" Ginger asked.

"She did, madam, but I was only to offer if you asked. Mrs. B. asked me to say that she couldn't get a piece of beef to roast from the butcher like you'd planned, and if there was something else you prefer. . . If not, she got some nice chops, and she wants to know if those would do."

"That would be splendid," Ginger said. "By the way, Lizzie, did you end up going to the circus?"

"Oh yes, last night with my family. It was thrilling, madam, though my stomach almost fell to my feet when those tigers came out. I'd never seen such creatures in real life before."

"Who was acting as ringmaster?"

"Who, madam?"

"What did the ringmaster look like?"

Lizzie's eyes went blank as she remembered. "A

roundish man with a bulbous nose. His outfit didn't seem to fit him very well."

Mr. Quill.

"Nanny, you don't mind taking Rosa from me now?"

Nanny Green, who'd been busy folding baby clothes and tidying up, rubbed her palms on her white apron and approached. "Of course not, madam."

Talk of the circus stirred Ginger's resolve to get to the bottom of this mystery, and not even Rosa's cute, chubby face could keep her from returning to the circus grounds at the soonest possible moment. If Inspector Sanders had interviewed the other people of interest—namely Mr. Rhimes and Mr. Singh—she'd have missed her chance to eavesdrop. There was no law saying she couldn't just talk to them herself under the guise of a worried mother.

BRINGING her Crossley to a dusty stop in the empty street around the circus tents, Ginger headed inside with determination. To blend in, she wore an understated grey frock with plain low pumps and a felt hat with the decorative silk floral piece removed.

Ginger had hoped the guard at the door would

be someone she was acquainted with, but alas, it was a new face.

"Hello," she said with a bright smile. "I'm a friend of Mr. Quill's. He told me to call in should I be in the area."

The worker looked Ginger up and down, and before he could deny her entry, she added, "I'm Lady Gold."

"Ah, good mornin', my lady," the man said, stepping aside.

Unsurprisingly, Ginger found Mr. Quill in the main tent giving orders, pointing short white fingers.

Smiling and waving a gloved hand, Ginger called out. "Mr. Quill!"

The former King of Clowns didn't return the smile. "Mrs. Reed." His gaze went to the door, and he scowled at the poor fellow who'd fallen victim to Ginger's charms.

"Congratulations on your first night as ringmaster!" Ginger clapped her gloved hands. "I'm told the evening went well."

"I'm happy to hear the talk about town is favourable," Mr. Quill said. "Now, as you can imagine, we're all very busy here and have no time for idle chatter."

"Of course," Ginger said. "I only came with a

message for my son's cousin, Marvin." The excuse was fabricated. "I know where he is. I promise I'll be quick." Ginger waved her fingers and turned toward the back of the tent.

"Mrs. Reed, I—" Mr. Quill was interrupted by a tattooed lady who apparently had an issue to resolve before he could stop Ginger from slipping behind the tent flap and out of sight.

The circus area was vast, and one could easily find oneself quite alone between show hours.

Or almost alone. In an empty passage between a tent and a grouping of caravans, the sound of a short-gaited person caught her attention. When she turned the corner, she found the little man.

"Prince?" Ginger said.

Prince turned and wrinkled his forehead. "Madam? Are you lost?"

"In fact, I am. I'm looking for Mr. Rhimes."

"Ah . . ." The little man's eyes darted about as he kicked at the dirt with the toe of his well-worn shoe.

Ginger cocked her head. "Is there something about Mr. Rhimes you'd like to tell me?"

"I'm not one to gossip, madam," Prince said, "but considering the dreadful circumstances . . ."

"You can tell me anything, Prince Natukunda. I promise to keep your confidence."

"I believe you, madam." He craned his neck to stare up. "Bancroft and Rhimes had a terrible row the day before Bancroft died. They thought they were alone, but people don't tend to notice when I'm around."

"Did you hear what the row was about?"

"No, I only caught the tail end, but I did hear Rhimes say he wished Bancroft had died instead of Mabel."

"Who's Mabel?"

"Rhimes' former acrobatic partner. She was married to Bancroft."

"I see," Ginger said, intrigued. "What happened to Mrs. Bancroft?"

"She fell from the wire, right at Bancroft's feet."

"An Accident?" Ginger asked.

"No, madam. She'd been humiliated after learning Bancroft had been involved in a string of affairs. Just before Mrs. Bancroft fell, she turned to Rhimes and said, "I'm sorry, but I just can't go on.""

"How sad."

The prince stared up, inclining his head. "Rhimes really fancied Mabel. Poor bloke. Broke his miserable heart when she married Bancroft, then again when she died."

"How awful for Mr. Rhimes."

"It was a terrible time for us all. Mrs. Bancroft was the sweetest soul. Such foul fate that she'd been wooed and deceived by a man like Bancroft."

Ginger couldn't help but feel pity for the wire walker. Such a horrible story and a sad loss. Unfortunately, it gave Mr. Rhimes a motive. And a strong motive for another man would take the spotlight off Scout. It was a simple matter of providing a measure of doubt.

"Where could I find Mr. Rhimes?" Ginger asked.

"The acrobats' tents are in the west corner." Prince pointed to a group of dirty white tents. "The one with the little red flag is Rhimes'. Perhaps he is there."

"Thank you, Prince," Ginger said. "Oh, please forgive my manners. How are you?"

Prince's expression softened. "It's been trying. Everyone is on pins and needles thinking a murderer is walking amongst us."

"I'm certain the culprit will be brought to light soon," Ginger said. "And everyone will be able to relax again."

"I do hope so, madam," Prince said. He bowed, then hurried away.

Prince had been correct. Ginger found the wire

walker in his tent, a small space with a camp bed, a table, one chair, and a heavily draped coat rack, which appeared to stand in for a wardrobe.

"Good day, Mr. Rhimes," Ginger said at the man's startled expression. "I hope I haven't caught you at an inconvenient time."

Mr. Rhimes stroked his moustache. "No time is convenient, Mrs. Reed. I'm surprised you've been allowed in durin' closin' hours."

Ginger ignored the challenge. "I'm worried about my son, Mr. Rhimes. His reputation is at stake."

"I would think he could lose more than that."

Although it was a cruel statement, the lithe man hadn't delivered it cruelly. "I do hope they get to the bottom of things," he added. "But I don't see how I can help you. I've already given my statement to the police."

Undaunted, Ginger pulled out her ace. "I'm sorry to hear about your acrobatics' partner, Mr. Rhimes. Wire walking is a dangerous sport."

Rhimes' demeanour turned to ice. "We know the risks."

"She was married to Mr. Bancroft when she died, was she not?"

Rhimes stepped forward, pointing a finger. "Bancroft was scum, and I'm not sorry he's dead. But it wasn't me who killed him. Mrs. Reed, I have no obligation to speak with you about it. Kindly leave."

The wire walker's swinging emotions hadn't surprised Ginger. She stepped back as she slipped her hand into her handbag and gripped the Remington inside. "Certainly. I'm sorry for upsetting you." Stopping at the tent entrance, she added, "Oh, Mr. Rhimes, did you mention to Inspector Sanders that you and Mr. Bancroft had argued on the night of his death?"

Instead of answering, Mr. Rhimes whipped his hat off his head, smacked it against a post, and stormed out with the cap gripped in his fist.

16

The maze of makeshift corridors amongst the tents and lean-tos had Ginger feeling a bit turned around, but when she heard the chimpanzees' rumble calls and a response from one of the elephants, she knew she was headed in the right direction.

As she entered the tent enclosure, her eyes were locked on her destination. The appearance of a slight young man caught her off guard, and she slammed into him, nearly knocking the lad off his feet.

"Oh, forgive me," Ginger said. "I wasn't looking where I was going."

The mime stared back with a round-eyed, startled expression. "It's my fault," he said, his voice cracking. "I'm used to moving about without making a sound. Please excuse me."

The mime seemed rushed, but Ginger didn't want to let a serendipitous opportunity pass.

"Kiki, wait."

The mime stopped, then turned slowly with reluctance. "I'm in rather a hurry."

"Yes, I won't keep you," Ginger said. "I just wanted to ask you about the other night."

The mime kept his eyes to the ground, his discomfort in her presence evident. Ginger mused as to why a shy person would gravitate to such a role, especially if they were determined to be a clown.

"My son, Scout, has mentioned you," Ginger said. "I know he wasn't around for very long, but I appreciate your effort to befriend him."

Kiki's eyes glistened, and for a moment, they reminded Ginger of someone, but for the life of her, she couldn't think of whom.

"Both of us are new," the mime said. "It's natural we'd cling together."

"Well, he appreciated it, as do I." Sensing the mime's impatience, Ginger added quickly, "Did you and Mr. Bancroft ever have a, shall we say, an unfortunate encounter?"

"No, madam. I haven't been around long enough

even to get noticed by the ringmaster. I'm rather invisible to some people."

The prince had made a similar statement, and the answer didn't exactly clear the mime. This oversight, being made to feel invisible, could've turned the mime against the ringmaster.

"Did you see anything that night, Kiki?" As he'd inferred, the mime had a way of sneaking about without calling attention to himself. Ginger continued, "Anything that could prove Scout's innocence?"

Kiki turned his head slowly. "I'm sorry I can't help, Mrs. Reed. Misfortune rains on the rich and poor, but not equally." He grabbed his stomach whilst wincing. "Please forgive me, madam, but nature calls."

"Yes, of course," Ginger said. "Thank you for your time."

Ginger let her gaze linger on the mime as he scampered away. Something about his eyes bothered her. And what did he mean by his strange comment, *Misfortune rains on the rich and poor, but not equally?* Surely the mime knew nothing of Scout's connection with Ginger's wealth, at least he hadn't at the time of Mr. Bancroft's' death.

As she continued to the elephant enclosure, Ginger was pleased to see Mr. Singh on the premises, though she had to look between tree-trunk-sized legs to find him.

"Mr. Singh?"

The animal trainer appeared from his position behind the largest of the beasts, the perpetrator, Tulip.

"Mrs. Reed?"

"Hello," Ginger said. "I hope I'm not disturbing you. How is Tulip this morning?"

Mr. Singh dusted his palms, his dark eyes filled with worry. "She's troubled, Mrs. Reed. She knows what she did and feels a tremendous amount of remorse."

Ginger knew that elephants were intelligent, but did they really have the capacity to experience empathy?

Mr. Singh seemed to read her mind. "Indeed, she has feelings. See how she drags her trunk about? She's despondent."

Ginger carefully approached, staying clear of the junior elephants and their protective mothers. Raising the back of her gloved hand and lightly placing it on Tulip's trunk, she whispered, "It'll be all right, Tulip."

"Will it?" Mr. Singh demanded. "Even though she was provoked, even though it was unintentional, she killed a man. The law won't stand for it."

"What will happen?" Ginger asked.

Mr. Singh turned his back on the elephants and lowered his voice. "A hunter's rifle will do the trick, I expect."

The animal trainer dug a dusty handkerchief from the pocket of his dungarees and dabbed at his eyes, streaking his brown cheeks with the effort.

Did it mean he hadn't killed Mr. Bancroft, or was he also suffering remorse, having used the elephant to kill his nemesis—his mind blind with rage, unable to think through the consequences?

"Who would do such a thing, Mr. Singh?" Ginger asked.

He let out a frustrated sigh. "There are so many who despised Bancroft, myself included. I've racked my brains, going through every scenario. Who knew about the keys? Pretty much everyone who would know Bancroft well enough to expect him to take revenge on Tulip."

He spun and locked his brown eyes, burning with passion, with Ginger's. "The biggest question is this, Mrs. Reed—who would attack Bancroft and not care that Tulip, this beautiful, gentle creature, would be destroyed in the process?"

Ginger stared up at Tulip, her heart gripped with distress at the poor creature's future. Tulip didn't deserve this.

Turning to Mr. Singh, she asked, "Did you reach a conclusion? Do you know someone who would callously use Tulip to his own advantage?"

"I can't say for sure," Mr. Singh said. "But if I had to pick, I would pick Mr. Quill."

The King of Clowns? "Why would Mr. Quill want Luther Bancroft dead?"

"For the simple reason that Bancroft made working for the circus a misery. And Quill had aspirations to be the ringmaster."

"I get the impression that you don't like Mr. Quill either," Ginger said. "You don't believe things will be any different under his direction?"

"Not if he sacrificed Tulip to get there." Mr. Singh scowled. "A man who is unkind to animals can't be trusted."

17

*L*ater that evening, after the family had eaten dinner, Ginger and Basil lounged in the sitting room, each enjoying a glass of brandy in front of the fire burning brightly in the stone fireplace. Waterhouse's *Mermaid* seemed to smile down on them from the mantel. The mythical creature had an ethereal beauty and long red locks that protected her modesty. The painting had been a gift from Ginger's father to her mother, from whom Ginger had inherited her red hair. The painting often brought her mother to mind, with sentimental emotions of wishing she'd lived beyond Ginger's birth, at least long enough that Ginger could've had a chance to know her and remember her.

She sat opposite Basil in a matching wingback

chair, her feet resting on an ottoman and Boss curled up on her lap. Behind her, nightfall had darkened the tall windows. A mahogany side table with a crystal decanter half full of brandy was situated against the far wall.

Ginger pushed off her shoes using the opposite foot to slip out of the heel, then wiggled her free toes with appreciation. "There are far too many suspects."

Try as they might, she and Basil couldn't stay away from the topic of the circus tragedy for long. She described her interview with the animal trainer. "I just can't picture Mr. Singh as our killer."

"Bancroft was known to be cruel to the animals," Basil said. "Perhaps it's a case of the straw breaking the camel's back."

Ginger stretched out her fingers, admiring how the firelight reflected in the gems of her rings. "He *very* strongly implicated Mr. Quill."

"I understand the King of Clowns is enjoying a large promotion," Basil said. "Braxton went again last night as part of the investigation. He informed me that Quill's first outing as ringmaster was a wee bit shaky."

"Perhaps Mr. Quill hadn't anticipated having stage fright." Sipping her brandy as she rubbed Boss' ears, Ginger added, "Mr. Singh suggested that Luther Bancroft's tendency towards nastiness had soured the mood and made living and working at the circus unpleasant."

"So, Quill's motive is opportunity for advancement?"

"Apparently."

"What about the others?" Basil asked.

"Mr. Rhimes, the wire walker, has a strong motive. His partner in acrobatics, a woman named Mabel whom he apparently loved, was once married to Bancroft."

"Living in a circus must be strange," Basil observed.

"Living in close quarters with little opportunity to find long-term relationships elsewhere would certainly make it so," Ginger said. "Mr. Bancroft had eyes for another woman, and according to Mr. Rhimes, it broke Mabel's heart. So much so that she purposely plunged to her death during a rehearsal, landing at her husband's feet."

Basil whistled. "I can't believe I'm not on this case. Sanders is a good chap, but he's . . ."

"He's not as experienced as you, love, I know," Ginger said. "But I had the opportunity to observe him in action, and I can reassure you that he's quite good at his job."

"Of course," Basil said, glancing away. "I didn't mean to imply otherwise."

Ginger felt pity for her husband. He was like a horse at the gate who was not allowed to race. "Are you sure you want to discuss this?" she asked. "It's insensitive of me to keep bringing it up."

"I *absolutely* want to discuss it," Basil said with fire in his eyes. "Scout's life and his future are at stake."

Ginger sipped her brandy as she considered him. "According to Mr. Petrenko, the prince was slighted in the form of his pay. Mr. Bancroft paid him child's wages, less than his taller counterparts. It's a weak motive, and after speaking to him myself, I don't see him as culpable."

"After all that is coming to light about Bancroft's poor character," Basil started, "it's a wonder he hadn't been murdered before now."

Ginger had to agree. "However, despicable people have the right to live out their lives in this country, alongside the noble."

"What about that mime?" Basil asked.

"Kiki?"

Ginger and Basil turned to Scout's voice at the door.

"What are you doing up, love?" Ginger asked.

"I'm not sleepy."

Scout's dirty-blond hair stood up on one side, and Ginger noted that the legs of his pyjama bottoms were getting shorter as his thin form stretched out taller.

Scout continued, "Thought I'd get a biscuit and a glass of milk."

When Scout had first come to Hartigan House, it was as Ginger's ward, and he earned his keep by helping Mrs. Beasley, so he knew his way around the kitchen.

"Why are you talking about Kiki?" Scout pressed.

"We're trying to solve the mystery of the ringmaster's demise," Basil said, "and clear your name."

Scout stepped inside the sitting room. "But Kiki's my friend."

Ginger twisted to stare her son in the eyes. "And yet, he was the first to implicate you."

"He didn't mean it that way." Scout shrugged, digging his fists into his pockets. "He's just the honest sort."

Boss, roused at Scout's voice, jumped to the floor, and casually stretched out his back legs.

"Why don't you take Boss with you for a treat," Ginger said. "Then back to your room. And if you can't sleep, read a book."

Ginger stretched out her legs over the ottoman. She felt like retiring to read herself. Basil seemed to feel the same way as he finished the last of his drink and walked over to Ginger to take her empty glass.

"What about the chap with the hairy face?" Basil said. "It seemed to me that he and the dwarf are good friends. Perhaps they worked together?"

"I thought of that too," Ginger said, getting to her feet. "Mr. Petrenko was also a victim of ridicule at the hands of the ringmaster. Again, not enough to drive one to murder, I should think. Still, if they decided to take it upon themselves to right the wrongs for everyone who'd been demeaned, cheated, or otherwise mistreated by the ringmaster, I suppose it's possible. But would they really sacrifice an innocent boy like Scout, or an elephant like Tulip?"

"Who's to know?" Basil said with a shrug. "Let's sleep on it." He reached for Ginger's hand, and they walked along the marble-tile floor of the entranceway to the curving staircase and up the dark green carpet runner to their bedroom.

18

"*Y*ou know as well as I do that I can't discuss the details with you." Inspector Sanders sat at his desk at Scotland Yard across from Basil, the small, high window letting in a glimpse of the gloomy morning light. His eyebrows were furrowed in puzzlement.

"I know, I know," Basil said, "and I don't mean for you to break official protocol. I just want to—"

"I understand that he's your son and all, Chief Inspector, but be that as it may . . ." Inspector Sanders' chin jutted out in a look of pure resolve.

"Blast it, man. Can we not discuss it in general terms without going into detail?" Basil let out a frustrated breath. The attention to protocol and regulation that Sanders was displaying were the very things

Basil adhered to. His own principles were conspiring against him. "You'll forgive me, Inspector." Basil raised himself to his feet. "You're right. I shouldn't be asking."

Sanders tapped his pencil on the top of his desk. "All those in the employ of the circus 'ave now been questioned."

Basil hesitated briefly before reclaiming his chair, casting an eager glance Sanders' way. "Have you considered looking outside the category of those who work at the circus?"

"Of course, but we 'ave to start with those closest to the crime, so to speak. I think you know that." Sanders' voice carried a hint of impatience.

"And you're aware of your suspects' backgrounds and potential motives, say that Rhimes fellow, the wire walker?"

"I'm aware of the man and 'is motive."

Basil stared at Sanders, admiring yet irritated by the man whose virtue wasn't working in Basil's favour. Basil couldn't help himself and took another stab. "Petrenko, the one with the hair all over his face? He's an interesting chap, isn't he?"

"Yes, 'e is."

"From the Ukraine, isn't he?"

"Seems to be, yeah."

Basil leaned in. "You mean you suspect he may not be? Is he trying to hide his background?"

"That's not what I meant, Chief Inspector Reed," Sanders said with a swipe at his moustache. "I suspect 'e was born there, just as 'e said."

"One wonders what kind of life a young chap with such an affliction would have growing up in a place like that," Basil mused. "Probably got teased by his mates. He might have developed a keen sense of self-preservation, wouldn't you say?"

"I'm not sayin' anythin'," Sanders said stubbornly. His eyes shifted to the open door of his office as if willing Basil to get up and leave.

"Well then, what about that mime character?" Basil was undaunted. "Dressed up like a clown, but not really a clown. Always lurking about, not saying anything except in pantomime. What kind of person goes for that kind of job, eh?"

A look of relief came to Sanders' face when a young constable appeared at his door. "Telephone call for you, sir," he said.

Sanders moved away from his desk with renewed energy. "If you'll excuse me, sir."

"Certainly," Basil said. "I'll just wait here."

Sanders cleared his throat and adjusted his

waistcoat before walking through the door and disappearing down the corridor.

According to Basil's watch, it took Sanders seven minutes to return. The inspector worked his lips as he gazed at Basil.

"What is it?" Basil asked.

"Another body at the circus," Sanders replied. "You might as well come along."

GINGER COULD REARRANGE her duties to her household affairs and her role at Feathers & Flair to chase after clues in the murder of Luther Bancroft, but she couldn't bring herself to cancel on her own family. At present, she was participating in a prearranged afternoon tea with Ambrosia and Felicia in the back garden, a delightful space with a well-kept lawn, a flower garden that bloomed nine months of the year, and a dense privacy hedge. A tray with tea and small sandwiches sat on the patio table.

"How is poor Scout faring?" Felicia asked. "Such a horrible turn of events."

"He likes to keep to his room," Ginger said. "He's mortified to be accused of such a heinous crime, as we all are for him. I'm very eager to have the real killer revealed."

"Poor thing," Felicia repeated.

After a tentative sip of tea, Ambrosia said, "I suppose it shouldn't come as too much of a surprise, considering his upbringing."

Ginger was aghast. "Grandmama!"

"I'm only saying what everyone is thinking, Ginger. The first few years of a child's life are fundamental. Right and wrong, social etiquette, propriety, it's ingrained early if not actually inborn." After a dainty sniff, she added, "His bad behaviour isn't that surprising, but it still reflects badly on the family name."

"Thankfully, for you," Ginger returned stiffly, "my family name is no longer Gold."

"More tea?" Felicia said brightly. She lifted the pot and poured without overt invitation. "Let's discuss more pleasant matters, shall we? Ginger, did you hear that a Ritz Hotel is opening in Boston?"

Ginger had, but her response to Felicia was delayed because her mind was busy sifting through the negative emotions brought on by Ambrosia's seemingly throwaway comment. Ginger had no doubt that Scout's predicament was the talk of the town. She'd been avoiding the newspapers for that very reason. One couldn't help what others thought, prone as most were to grab onto gossip before the facts could be presented. One could only keep one's chin up, which Ginger did with the thought. She twisted a strand of her red bob with one finger, ensuring its tip was situated just under a cheekbone where she had applied rouge earlier for a healthy-looking glow.

"Ginger?" Felicia stared at Ginger, her thin dark brows arching seriously.

"Yes, right, I have heard," Ginger said. "It's an odd thought to imagine a European institution in America."

Ambrosia huffed. "Americans appear to want to have their cake and eat it too."

"What do you mean?" Ginger asked coolly.

"They wanted revolution, to separate themselves from king and country, yet they want to keep their district names like New England and cities like New York, and the like. They want our tea—"

Felicia cut in with a grin, "But not our whiskies."

"Imagine the Ritz without champagne," Ambrosia twittered. "It's like bread without butter or tea without biscuits."

Ginger couldn't disagree with her former grand-mother-in-law on that point.

"How are things going for you on the home front,

Felicia?" Ginger asked. "Have matters settled with members of your staff?"

Felicia stiffened at the subject change, her shoulders pushing back and her lips pushing out. "Burton is insufferable! He feigns hardness of hearing whenever I speak to him and in front of the rest of the staff. It's humiliating."

"What does Charles say?" Ginger asked.

Felicia pouted. "I haven't told him. They are so fond of each other. Burton is the faithful hound that bites at the heels of all newcomers."

"You're not afraid Charles will choose his butler over you, are you?" Ambrosia said with a note of indignation. "A wife is most certainly of higher rank than a butler."

"I'm quite aware, Grandmama," Felicia blustered miserably.

"You'll have to do something," Ginger said. "The longer you let this issue persist, the more difficult it will become to address it properly."

"I know," Felicia replied. Regaining her poise, she tidied her hair, pushing a dark strand behind her ear and patting the bottom of the bob. "Despite my outgoing personality, I really do despise confrontation and conflict."

"I can give you the name of a service to find a new butler," Ambrosia said.

Felicia stared ahead. "I do hope it doesn't come to that."

The French window opened, and Pippins stepped through. He had one hand behind his back and the other, in a white glove, holding up a silver tray.

"Forgive my intrusion, Mrs. Reed, but a message has come for you. The messenger boy said it was urgent. From Mr. Reed, madam."

A curious look was shared between the three ladies as Ginger rose to accept the note.

"Oh mercy."

"Good news or bad?" Felicia asked.

"Both," Ginger answered. "The bad news is there's been another murder at the circus. The good news is that our Scout is no longer a suspect."

19

Ginger skidded onto the street near the circus tents, the thin, rubber tyres of the car's white-spoked wheels spraying dust as she came to a stop. Adjusting her felt cloche hat, she hurried as quickly as a lady could to the entrance, only to be stopped by Horace Rhimes.

"Mrs. Reed," he said snidely. "Surely you must know the opening hours by now?"

"I've been summoned by my husband, Chief Inspector Basil Reed," Ginger said. "He's here, is he not?"

"It's all right, man."

Ginger turned to the familiar voice and smiled at the uniformed man. "Constable Braxton, hello."

Mr. Rhimes huffed with resignation and allowed Ginger to pass by. She continued her address with the constable. "Where might I find Chief Inspector Reed?"

"This way, madam," Constable Braxton said, turning on the heel of his black leather boots. "Follow me."

Ginger was getting the feel of the maze of alleyways that made up the living and storage areas at the back, but it was the first time she'd encountered this tent filled with props and sundry items.

Basil and Inspector Sanders, with grim expressions on their faces, were peering into a trunk, its rounded lid up and blocking Ginger's view of the contents.

Her arrival caught their attention, and Basil said, "I thought you'd like to be in on this."

"Quite right," Ginger said. Her heart dropped with the realisation that the corpse fitting in that trunk would have to be of diminutive size.

"Oh no, is it the prince?"

There was no need for anyone to answer as Ginger stepped up to the trunk and looked for herself. Poor Prince Natukunda, known once as Billy Smith, was in the trunk with his skin looking ghoulishly pale, a red gash marring one cheek. A hole in his trousers and a missing shoe indicated a possible struggle.

"What was the cause of death?" Ginger asked as the means wasn't immediately apparent.

Basil shone the beam of his torch on the prince's head. "There appears to be a contusion there. Perhaps he was struck."

"I've summoned the doctor," Inspector Sanders added. "'E should be 'ere in a jiff."

"Who found the body?" Ginger asked.

"Quill," Basil said. To Sanders, he added, "Shall we take this time to ask a few questions."

"Those are my thoughts, sir," Sanders returned, then instructed Braxton to bring Quill to them.

Basil added, "Might as well round up the others."

Mr. Quill must have been hovering nearby as he soon entered the props room. Chairs, set out of view from the trunk with the body inside, had been produced for the interview.

As Inspector Sanders was still officially leading the case, he took charge.

"Mr. Quill." He leaned forward in his chair. "You must be broken up about the sad loss of another of your own."

The new ringmaster took a white cloth out of his

pocket and wiped his forehead. "It's been a hard week."

"You won't mind if I ask you a few questions. I've requested that Chief Inspector Reed participate in the questioning with Mrs. Reed as an observer."

Mr. Quill lifted a shoulder. "Whatever it takes to get to the bottom of this. These deaths are bad for business."

Ginger stiffened at the man's lack of empathy. "They're bad for those who've been murdered as well."

"You've been with this circus for a long time now, is that right?" Inspector Sanders said.

"Since Mr. Sweeney started it just after the war," Mr. Quill snorted. *The world is ready for a diversion,* he liked to say."

"So, you know all the key players."

"Certainly."

"Who, in your estimation, had something against the prince?" Basil asked.

"No one. He was a novelty act. Didn't do much, really. No reason to want to kill him."

"He told me he was invisible amongst the crew," Ginger said. "People would often say or do things as if he wasn't even there."

Mr. Quill sniffed. "It's true, I gather. I stopped

seeing him years ago. All I know is I didn't kill him, and I don't know who did."

Inspector Sanders dismissed the former King of Clowns. Ginger didn't think the man was their killer as he didn't appear to have any signs of a physical altercation on his person., or have any apparent motive.

Mr. Petrenko disturbed the interview, stumbling into the props room.

"Is not true!" The fur on his face was dampened with his tears. "Tell me is not true!"

Inspector Sanders stood, bowing his head as he reluctantly gave the man the news. "I'm afraid so, Mr. Petrenko. Prince Natukunda is deceased."

Mr. Petrenko dropped to his knees and moaned. Ginger's heart broke for the man. It was clear the prince's friendship had meant a lot to him.

"I'm so sorry for your loss, Mr. Petrenko," she said. With wide eyes, she silently beseeched Basil to do something.

Basil nodded, then called for his constable. "Braxton. Take Mr. Petrenko back to his quarters and see if you can find a bit of whisky for him."

"Yes, sir." Constable Braxton helped the distraught man to his feet and guided him out. Ginger was eager to question the man about his good friend, but they needed to give him time to compose himself.

Mr. Rhimes was next. He *did* look beaten up. When she'd first arrived, Ginger hadn't paid note to the deepening bruise on the wire walker's cheek or the red marks on his forearms.

Inspector Sanders noticed his contusions too. "Mr. Rhimes, you look like you've been in a fight."

"Just with the net." Mr. Rhimes showed off his forearms. "Rope burns. Practisin' a new acrobatic routine. My timin' was out."

"When I spoke to Prince Natukunda, he told me that he'd witnessed a row between you and Mr. Bancroft," Ginger said. "Perhaps there was more to the story?"

"That stupid argument had nothin' to do with this!" Mr. Rhimes' neck grew red as his hands created fists, confirming the prince's claim that Mr. Rhimes was easily angered. "The novelty acts have nothin' to do but sneak around and gossip. Prince and his hairy friend were the worst, always natterin' and stickin' their noses in things that were none of their business."

"No need to get heated," Basil said with a note of warning. "Can you think of anyone who would want Prince Natukunda dead?"

"For starters, he wasn't no African prince," Mr. Rhimes said. "Englishman through and through. Plain ol' Billy Smith. And to answer your question, no. I don't see why you're wasting your time on him."

Ginger folded her arms and very nearly started tapping her toe. "For the same reason we'd waste time on you, Mr. Rhimes, should you ever find yourself in a similar unfortunate situation. Billy Smith was an English citizen and a human being."

Basil cast a disparaging look at Mr. Rhimes before saying, "You may go, but please don't leave the circus grounds."

Mr. Rhimes stormed away with an air of indignation, and before Inspector Sanders could call in the next person, the pathologist arrived.

This time, it wasn't Dr. Gupta but someone new, a youthful-looking man with ruddy cheeks and blond hair.

Basil began the introductions. "I'm Chief Inspector Reed." Motioning to Ginger he added, "And this is my wife, Mrs. Reed."

"Oh, hello! I'm Dr. Davidson." He gave Basil a hearty handshake and directed a friendly nod to Ginger. "How do you do! Dr. Gupta speaks very highly of you both."

Ginger was surprised by the announcement and

wondered why Dr. Gupta had never mentioned a colleague named Davidson.

Dr. Davidson answered her question for her. "I'm new to University Hospital. I'm Dr. Gupta's intern. He was tied up with another case, so he sent me instead."

The doctor followed Basil to the trunk, and Basil opened the lid.

Dr. Davidson shook his head as he came closer. "I understand this is the second murder in one week."

"We're eager to prevent more," Basil said.

Braxton returned and was followed by Kiki, who stuck his head through the tent door.

"You wanted to see me?"

Ginger stepped between Kiki and the body, opening the arms and the flaps of her flowing orange velvet spring coat to block the mime's view.

"Would you mind taking a seat over there?"

Kiki, as usual, was in full, thick face paint and costume. Ginger frowned as she noted he walked with a slight limp. "Have you hurt your leg?" she asked.

Kiki lowered himself onto the chair. "Stubbed my toe. No big deal."

Ginger smiled, wanting to put the mime at ease. "The inspector will be with you shortly."

Leaving the mime, she stepped up to Basil and whispered in his ear. "We need to see this Kiki fellow without his make-up."

"I concur," Basil said. Then to Inspector Sanders, he added, "While we're waiting on the doctor, do you mind if Braxton accompanies the mime to a washing station so that we might see his face?"

"Not at all. I think it's time," the inspector said.

Braxton nodded, understanding his task. "Come with me, Mr. Kiki."

"Why?" the mime asked firmly. "What do I have to do with it?"

"We just want to see your face, sir," Braxton said. He took the mime by the arm so there could be no misinterpretation. The mime pulled it away in a huff.

"No need for force," Kiki said. "I've no reason not to cooperate."

"All right then," Braxton returned as he accompanied the mime out of the tent.

Ginger gave her attention to Dr. Davidson, who examined the prince's scalp.

"Death appears to have been caused by a blow to

the head with a blunt object," he said. "By the size and shape of the injury, my guess would be the head of a hammer."

Inspector Sanders groaned, "There are plenty of 'ammers about."

Ginger thought of all the structures built and torn down every time the circus moved from town to town. It would be like looking for a black cat at midnight.

"He struggled with his attacker before the final blow," Dr. Davidson continued. "There are finger-shaped bruises on his forearms. Someone gripped him tightly. Scrapes on his shins. A broken toe on the foot with a missing shoe.

"So, we're lookin' for someone with defensive wounds, 'oo is also in possession of an 'ammer," Inspector Sanders said. "I'll send our officers on a search, though it feels a bit like a fool's errand."

Dr. Davidson, squatting by the trunk, had the dead man's hand in his own. "He has something under his fingernails." He removed a scraping apparatus from his black doctor's bag and dragged it under the right forefinger. Using a magnifying glass, he examined the matter he'd extracted. "Looks like face paint."

"Could be any one of the many clowns," Basil

said. He cast a glance at Ginger who was working her lips. "What is it, love?"

"Something Mr. Rhimes said, or more how he said it. That the novelty acts don't mind their own business, his implication being that they tend to snoop on others. Prince once confessed to me that he felt invisible, and that people would say things around him they might not otherwise."

Basil raised a brow. "Blackmail?"

"Prince was upset, and rightly so, about not being paid the same as his taller colleagues. Perhaps he found a little blackmail helped to make up the difference."

"I'll get the constables to check his quarters for a ledger."

Ginger smiled. "Not all criminals keep a financial record of their crimes. And I doubt we're talking big numbers. Just a couple of quid here and there."

"Hardly worth killing over."

Ginger pushed a loose lock of red hair behind her ears. "It would depend on the secret, wouldn't it?"

20

The more time Ginger spent at the circus amongst the many tents and trailers, the more she began to understand that the circus village wasn't one big happy family. It was broken into several community sectors and had its own class system, the ringmaster being on the top of the pyramid. Underneath him were the acrobats, then the animal acts, the clowns, the workmen, and finally the novelty acts.

Even amongst the novelty acts, a certain amount of classification took place. Those who had natural but unusual talents such as the jugglers, the unicyclist, and the sword swallower were more valued than those born with an abnormality, such as the Siamese twins, the tattooed lady—who had tattooing to cover large and unbecoming birthmarks on her face and torso—and the contortionist, a lady born with extraordinarily long limbs and joint hyper-mobility.

Then, of course, there were Dmytro Petrenko and the prince.

When Ginger and Basil entered the tent where the novelty acts had gathered, the place grew silent. It was as if the magical mysteries of the circus world had reversed itself, and the social outcasts were now the normal folk, and Ginger and Basil were the odd ones to be stared at.

The tattooed lady wore a silk kimono tied loosely around a tiny waist; one could hardly tell where the pattern on her robe ended and the one on her legs started. She let out a column of smoke from the cigarette she'd been puffing on. "You must be lost."

"Indeed, we are not," Basil said. "I'm Chief Inspector Reed and this is, er, Lady Gold of Lady Gold Investigations."

The moniker came in handy when they found themselves on the same case. A married couple doing the same work could come across as odd, and suspects often didn't respect it.

"Ohh," moaned the contortionist. Ginger hadn't registered her presence at first, as her legs and arms were wrapped around her body like a knotted bow tie. "You're here about poor Prince." One leg unfolded like an insect limb—the leg of her modern, wide-legged trousers falling to her ankles—followed by an arm. "We're all simply devastated."

"And you are?" Ginger asked.

"Priscilla." Priscilla freed her remaining limbs, stretched out her rather long body, then joined the tattooed lady at the table. The rest of the people in the room slowly cleared out, one by one. "Don't mind them," Priscilla said. "They're shy."

"I'm Dee-Dee," the tattooed lady said. "We're shattered to hear about Prince." Her face looked like a map of the stars with a starburst etched above one eye. It rippled into folds when she raised a brow. "Who would do such a terrible thing?"

"That's what we're hoping to find out," Basil said.

After lighting her own cigarette Priscilla asked, "Do you want a chair? I can round one up."

"That's quite all right," Ginger said. "We shan't be long. Do you know if Prince had any enemies at the circus?"

"None!" Priscilla said. She exchanged her cigarette for a handkerchief and dabbed at her eye. "Prince was a darling. We all loved him."

"Well," Basil started, "not everyone did, apparently. Did he happen to have a falling-out with anyone recently?"

The contortionist blew her nose, her pointy elbows jutting out to each side like wings. "I don't think so."

"Did Prince ever keep secrets?" Ginger asked gently. "For money?"

Dee-Dee laughed lightly. "He did. Everyone knew it."

Ginger and Basil shared a startled look.

"He was blackmailing people?" Basil clarified. "And everyone at the circus knew it?"

"It wasn't *real* blackmail," Dee-Dee said. "It started off as a joke, you know, because Prince got short-changed on payday—" She frowned before adding, "I can't say I'm sorry to see Bancroft go, the cheapskate. Anyway, Prince said he'd keep our secrets safe in exchange for a little *supplement*."

"And everyone was all right with that?" Basil asked with a note of doubt in his voice.

"They were," Dee-Dee said. "They weren't real secrets."

"Can you give us an example?" Ginger asked.

Dee-Dee and Priscilla stared at each other for a moment before Priscilla shrugged, her eyes now dry.

"Well, Joe, the juggler," Priscilla offered, "he'd sneak more than his fair share of the bacon on bacon days."

"And Max—he does the sword-swallowing trick —he has *special* tastes." Dee-Dee delivered this titbit with a wink. "Boudoir photographs from France."

"Anne and Alice, they're the twins, Alice fancied one of the workmen—"

Dee-Dee interrupted, "Ohh, Mr. Barney. He's delish!"

Priscilla grinned as if she agreed. "Alice would've died if Prince had told Mr. Barney how she felt." She added hurriedly, "But Prince would never do that. It was all in fun."

"To help even out the pay discrepancy," Basil said.

Dee-Dee nodded. "That's right."

"Did he ever 'keep secrets' about people not part of the novelty acts?" Ginger asked. She'd seen Prince in action and witnessed the anger that Horace Rhimes had exhibited over what he called spying and gossip.

Priscilla shook her head, her long neck twisting. "Dmytro warned him not to do that. 'Don't bother the uppers' he said."

"The 'uppers'?" Basil asked.

"Yeah, the talent," Dee-Dee said. "You know, the

acrobats and clowns . . ." Dee-Dee's eyes widened and her red lips fell open, changing the galaxy printed on her face. "Oh no. Did he, though? Did he catch a secret about an upper? Is that why he got killed?"

Basil held out a palm. "We're in the early stages of our investigation, miss. There's no need to jump to conclusions."

Priscilla stubbed out her cigarette. "I just don't know if I feel safe anymore."

Dee-Dee huffed. "It's not like we can go anywhere else. We'll just have to watch each other's backs."

Ginger and Basil thanked the women and left. As far as Ginger was concerned, the tattooed lady had it right. It was likely that Prince had learned something about one of the "uppers" and it had got him killed.

21

"*There he is!*"

Ginger pointed at the lithe figure of Horace Rhimes at the opposite end of the crowded corridor running between tents where they now found themselves. They'd agreed that the angry acrobat would be a good next suspect to interview.

Basil shouted, "Mr. Rhimes!"

The man hesitated briefly, then ducked through a tent flap. Ginger placed a gloved hand on her hat as she raced after Basil, already several strides ahead of her as he chased Mr. Rhimes.

"Rhimes!"

Anyone found to be in their way scampered out of sight or thinned their bodies against the trailer walls so Ginger and Basil could shimmy past them.

Police, Ginger found, had a special skill when it came to dispersing people.

Basil eased through the tent flap that Mr. Rhimes had slipped through, Ginger following him, and they found themselves once again in the back of the big tent. Empty of the vivacious crowds of the last performance, the unoccupied seats, abandoned booths, and unmoving streamers gave the oversized space an eerie, haunted feeling.

"Blast!" Basil muttered. "The blighter's eluded us."

Ginger held a finger to her lips, sensing they were not alone. As she scanned the empty seats and the darkened stalls, the smell of dust and musky wood filled her nostrils. Then slowly she looked up. There, high up on the tiny platform in front of the wire, stood Mr. Rhimes.

She waved. "Hello there, Mr. Rhimes."

"I'm in the middle of rehearsin'," Mr. Rhimes said stiffly. "I shan't come down."

"This is a murder investigation, Rhimes," Basil said. "We'll simply have to wait for you to finish."

"Do what you must." Rhimes grasped a wooden balancing rod then positioned it horizontally in front of his body, holding it with both hands.

"We can continue our interview from here," Ginger said, "if you prefer."

"Again, whatever you feel you must do." Mr. Rhimes took a step onto the wire, and it swayed with the motion. Ginger held her breath. The safety net, normally held along the edges by several clowns, lay flat on the ground. If Mr. Rhimes fell, they could be looking at a third circus death.

"You had better come down," Basil said. "You do realize there's no one to hold the net for you."

Mr. Rhimes took another step, his full weight now on the wire. "I am a professional, Chief Inspector Reed. I shall not fall."

Basil huffed at the man's hubris and Ginger shared his frustration. However, one couldn't control the foolish actions of another. With a loud voice Basil said, "Was Mr. Natukunda blackmailing you?"

After another step, Mr. Rhimes said, "Prince was blackmailin' everyone. Quite a scheme he had going on."

"We're told by members of the novelty acts that it was all a bit of fun," Ginger said. "Until, it appears, it wasn't?"

Mr. Rhimes said nothing, stepping silently with quick dance-like steps until he reached the opposite platform. With the security of the wooden structure firmly beneath him, Mr. Rhimes stared down on Ginger and Basil's heads. "That little runt and his hairy sidekick were a nuisance, but of late, the dwarf had become a menace. Got a little greedy, he did."

Without waiting for the next question, Mr. Rhimes stepped back onto the wire, this time with more ease than the last.

"What secret did he learn of yours?" Basil asked. "It's clear that he'd made you angry. You might as well tell me. I'll find out eventually."

"What are most bribes about, Chief Inspector?" Mr. Rhimes returned. "Money." He took a careful step. "Women." Another step. "And money."

Ginger had a solid kink in her neck at this point and applied a bit of pressure with two fingertips. "You said money twice."

"Indeed," Mr. Rhimes said, his life spared again as he reached the platform from which he'd begun. "It's twice as often the case, but in mine . . ." He shook out his shoulders and lifted his chin. "Mine wasn't money, and that's all I'm prepared to say about it."

"Is there anyone who could verify your claims?" Basil said.

Mr. Rhimes sniffed. "You could ask Barney."

"Mr. Barney?" Ginger said. "The workman?"

The acrobat narrowed his eyes, his gaze burrowing into hers. "You know him?"

"Oh, no. It's just his name has come up in our investigation."

Mr. Rhimes looked truly alarmed. "Barney has nothing to do with any of this. He's not even a regular part of the circus. He barely knew Bancroft or the dwarf."

Ginger wondered if the man was protesting too much.

"But, if I were you—" Unbelievably, the acrobat appeared to lose his balance. In a split second, Mr. Rhimes let out a yelp then shouted, "Watch out below!"

Ginger and Basil sprang out of the way, the balancing bar clattering to the ground between them.

Oh mercy!

Fearing the worst, Ginger searched for the man's broken body on the dust, but then heard his chuckle from high above, where he swung upside down, his knees latched over the wire like a child hanging off a tree limb.

With a hand to her chest, she shouted, "Mr. Rhimes!"

"I'm all right, I'm all right," he returned with reassurance. "Just a bit of fun."

Basil bristled. "I can assure you, Rhimes, that a murder investigation is not the time or place for games. I could have you arrested for obstruction!"

"Very well, be like that." Mr. Rhimes, with admirable abdominal strength reached up to grab the wire with both hands, then twisted in such a way that he now had his legs wrapped around it, as if it were a thread running through the eye of a needle.

"Like I was sayin'" Rhimes began, as he pulled his way along the wire, grasping it in front of him, one fist at a time.

"Yes?" Basil said with impatience, then added wryly, "Don't leave us hanging."

"I'd look into Leonard Quill."

"We already know his motive for killing Bancroft," Basil said, "but why would he want Prince Natukunda dead?"

"Like I already told you, Prince liked to eaves-drop and snitch." Mr. Rhimes reached the end of the wire and, with very little effort, hoisted himself onto the platform.

"What secret of Mr. Quill's did Prince know?" Ginger asked.

"Quill enjoyed a stretch of His Majesty's hospitality."

"Is that so?" Basil asked.

"Indeed. Not somethin' Quill likes the general public to know. And he'd do anythin' to keep from going back to prison."

"What did Prince want from Mr. Quill for keeping quiet?" Ginger asked.

"The dwarf thought Quill would treat him better than Bancroft, and pay him equally," Rhimes answered. "When he didn't, Prince threatened to go to the police."

"With evidence that Quill killed Bancroft?" Basil asked.

"That's the thing," Mr. Rhimes said. "I don't think he had anythin' on Quill. I think he was bluffin'."

*a*s Ginger and Basil searched for the King of Clowns, now Ringmaster, Ginger's thoughts lingered on Horace Rhimes and his silly falling stunt. She couldn't help but wonder if the man was insane, but even if he was, was he crazy enough to commit two murders?

As they headed back to the clowns' quarters, Basil said, "I find it noteworthy that Quill failed to mention Natukunda's bribery attempt."

"Not if he wanted to keep his police record under wraps," Ginger said. "He'd only just been promoted to ringmaster, and he didn't want to mar his reputation. There's also the fact that Prince had face paint under his nails . ."

"Is Quill still clowning?" Basil asked. "I'd think

he'd give that up with his new role. Perhaps we're heading in the wrong direction."

Ginger slowed. "You might be right. Unless there's a reason he'd go back to using face paint. A guise? Let's ask someone where we might find him."

The thing with the circus, it seemed, was that when one wasn't looking for anybody specifically, there were hordes of people milling about, but when one wanted to find someone, even to just ask directions, one found oneself alone.

"We're bound to find someone eventually," Ginger said. "I believe many members of the troupe sleep during the day." She caught sight of a colourful shirt. "Oh, there's someone." Louder she called out, "Cooee!"

To her surprise, the person who turned was Dmytro Petrenko. Ginger whispered to Basil, "Serendipitous encounter."

"Hello, Mr. Petrenko," Basil said. "You're just the man we were hoping to run into."

Mr. Petrenko had the look of a beaten man. His eyes were downcast, the hair on his face damp and oily, and his shoulders turned inwards. "I do not know anything," he said.

"Perhaps I should ask a question first," Basil

returned. "I understand you and Prince Natukunda were good friends."

Mr. Petrenko sniffed. "The best."

"I'm so sorry for your loss," Ginger said kindly. "It's so terribly difficult when one loses a beloved."

"It is, madam."

"I'm afraid I need to ask you about Prince's propensity for bribery," Basil said. "We've been told it started out as a bit of fun, everyone playing along to support the pay discrepancy."

"That is right," Mr. Petrenko said. "Bancroft was a nasty so-and-so, if you know what I mean. He had no right, but Prince, well, he had no power."

"Had Prince discovered a new secret?" Ginger asked. "Did he confide in you?"

"Well, madam, he most certainly did. Just yesterday he—he was very excited—he told me he had good one on the mime."

"Did he tell you what it was?" Ginger asked.

"No, we got interrupted, and then—" Mr. Petrenko shrank into himself again.

"Did he ever have anything on you?" Basil asked.

"No, sir. I am boring man. And Prince would not do that to me. We were friends."

"Thank you, Mr. Petrenko," Basil said. "We'll find you if we need you again."

. . .

THEY REACHED the tent the clowns used to get ready, which smelled sour from perspiration and greasepaint. A metal rack held all manner of bright costumes. Bins and shelves were stocked with shoes and hats.

With his hands behind his back, Constable Braxton examined a row of photographs of the clowns. The space was limited, and they had to circumvent stacked chairs, foldable tables, and more racks of clothing.

"Where is the mime?" Basil asked. Ginger had nearly forgotten that Basil had sent Constable Braxton to keep an eye Kiki.

"Just in there, sir." Braxton pointed to a wooden barrier that had a sign painted over a doorway, "Water Closet and Washing Stations." Braxton continued, "He had to use the loo before washing off his paint."

Basil knocked on the door. "Kiki! Come out. We need to ask a few questions." Basil turned the handle when the mime failed to respond immediately, but it failed to give way.

"It's locked," he said, then hammered on the door with the flat side of his fist. "You in there. It's the police. Open up!"

"Let me at it, sir," Braxton said. He was about to ram it with his shoulder—a manoeuvre Basil knew was ineffective at worst and extremely painful at most—when Ginger stepped up with a set of lock picks in her hand.

"Allow me?" she asked.

Basil immediately stepped aside. He no longer questioned Ginger's unique set of skills, though they never failed to amaze and impress him. Within seconds the door was open.

Inside was a bank of six metal washbasins along the left wall with brightly lit mirrors. Jars of paint and make-up brushes sat on the wooden counter. There was no one sitting at any of them. The room was closed in with no windows or external doors. On the right were two doors marked WC. Basil quickly knocked sharply on one while Ginger knocked on the other. Upon receiving no response, they both opened the doors simultaneously.

Both cubicles were empty, but for a small pile of discarded clothing on the floor.

Constable Braxton lifted his helmet and scratched his head. "Where'd he go?"

Ginger stepped closer, bending at the knees to take a closer look at the dirty laundry. With two fingers, she picked up the end of a piece of cotton binding material. Standing, the strip of fabric lifted with her, the length of it reaching the floor.

Basil wrinkled a brow. "What is it?"

Instead of answering, Ginger turned to the police officer. "Constable Braxton, did you see anyone else while you were waiting?"

"Only a young lady, sir," Braxton said. "She was lost."

"Did you see her actually come into this tent?" Ginger asked.

Braxton stiffened. "Well, no, I had my back turned to the door. I was admiring these clown photos. There was a noise, something fell, so I investigated, and when I turned around, she was there."

"What did she look like?" Basil asked.

"She was young and slim, early twenties, I would say. Dressed quite nicely in a blue dress and black hat."

"Can you tell us anything more?" Ginger said. "What colour was her hair, for example?"

Constable Braxton thought for a moment. "The hat was one of those cloche kinds, pulled down, and her hair must've been short and tucked underneath. She never really looked me in the eye, so I can't say for sure what colour her eyes were, but I couldn't help but notice her freckles. She had lots of 'em on her nose and cheeks."

Ginger's mind raced. Could the mime Kiki be a female passing as a young male? It would explain the binding material. She could have stowed the blue dress in a hidden spot in anticipation of a time she would need a quick change.

Could she be . . .

Her fears were confirmed when they ran into Marvin in the corridor.

"I just found these." Marvin held up several small notes. "I 'appened to notice the end of one of 'em stickin' out from pillow on the camp bed Scout slept on."

Ginger and Basil read the notes together.

You were born special, like me.
Your parents don't understand.

Ginger stared at the notes then shot a look at Basil. "That sharp, left-leaning cursive," she said hoarsely as if the implication had stolen her breath.

Basil swallowed hard and removed a note from his wallet.

Dear Chief Inspector I Reed,

You haven't seen the last of me.
Vera

Ginger pinned Basil with a steely gaze. "Where did you get that."

"It came to me by messenger. I didn't want to worry you."

Ginger didn't have time to identify her emotions —anger, frustration, mistrust—before Marvin handed them a third note. Her chest felt cinched in a vice grip as she read it.

Don't worry! I know where to find you.

Ginger held both notes side by side. "It's the same person, Basil. Kiki is Vera Sharp, and she's after Scout!"

23

*S*cout lay on his bed and stared at the ceiling. His mind went back to when he'd been simply a ward rather than a son, and his bedroom was one floor higher in the attic where Pippins and Mrs. Beasley had rooms. He once had to take the narrow and long stairs that opened to the kitchen; he now ran up and down the broad curved staircase with its polished rail—a task once given to him—and the plush carpet underfoot.

His fortunes had turned for the better, like no one else he'd known. Look how quick he was to throw it all away.

Not only had he the comfort of his dreams, but he had the love and support of two parents—people dedicated to his health, safety, and education. Here he had leisure time for horses, tennis, and cricket, as well as the companionship of Boss.

Sensing Scout's growing unease, the Boston terrier nuzzled in under his arm. He took his role of comforter seriously. "You're such a good doggie, Boss," Scout whispered as he patted the dog's short black snout. "Not like me. I've been a frightful dunce."

Scout felt like his world had been tipped upside down and rattled and that he was solely to blame. He only hoped that it would be positioned upright and in its proper order when the pieces all landed.

Boss' head snapped up, his ears stiffened and pointed towards the door.

"What is it, boy?"

Boss barked then jumped off the bed. He nosed the bedroom door open and ran onto the landing, where he perched on his haunches.

Scout followed.

There was someone at the door. Pippins opened it and spoke, though Scout couldn't understand what was being said.

After a moment, a lady dressed in a floral frock that hung low at the waist stepped inside and followed Pippins to the sitting room. Pippins opened the French doors and said something to the lady, who disappeared inside. Then, to Scout's surprise, instead of heading to the kitchen in search of a maid to bring tea, Pippins headed up the stairs.

Scout didn't want to look as if he was spying, so he hurried to his room. Pippins must be in search of someone else.

Again, Scout was surprised by Pippins' knock on his bedroom door. What could he want?

"Hello?" Scout said.

"Begging your pardon, young master," Pippins began. There was a time when Scout had taken orders from the butler, but Pippins had handled the change in his status as admirably as one could hope for, unlike other staff members or some of the family.

"A Miss Spalding is waiting in the sitting room, a friend of your mother's family from America. She would very much like to meet you."

"From America?" Scout said. "And she wants to meet me?"

"Yes, indeed. Apparently, Mrs. Reed writes regularly and speaks often and highly of you."

Scout wasn't interested in spending time with an old person from America, but he really didn't have anything else to do and was rather bored. It wouldn't hurt to say hello.

"All right, then," he said. He flew down the staircase, much more quickly than old Pips could manage, and breezed into the sitting room.

Miss Spalding wore a pretty frock, a wide-brimmed hat, and held the handles of a handbag with white gloves. She rose to her feet when Scout entered the room and offered her hand.

"My, my, it is such an honour to meet you, young man," the lady said as Scout returned her handshake

He noticed she had a firm grip.

Miss Spalding had an accent that Scout had only heard a few times in his life, mostly whilst working on the steamships. He guessed she was from somewhere like Boston or New York.

As she spoke, Scout realised that she wasn't an old lady, but rather young, like Aunt Felicia, pretty with a slender figure. He'd noticed these kinds of things about girls and ladies lately. A smattering of freckles on her nose and cheeks added to her attraction. Her smiling and unflinching gaze made him blush, which irritated him.

"How do you do?" he said.

"Just dandy, now that I'm here in good old London." She carefully pulled off a glove, turned it inside out, dropped it into her handbag, and performed the strange routine with the second glove. "Won't your father just be so surprised!"

"My mum, you mean," Scout said.

"Oh, yes." Miss Spalding waved a bare hand, sending a whiff of her floral perfume. "A slip of the tongue."

Scout felt overwhelmed, and a little confused at how being alone in close quarters with a female made him overheat. He wiped sweaty palms on his trousers and cringed when he saw that Miss Spalding had seen him do it, her eyes flashing with something other than delight.

Her eyes returned to his face, and her face softened into a smile.

"I'm adopted too, you see. I grew up on the streets of Boston but was adopted right around the same age as you. So naturally, I'm taken with your story. We're like twins!"

She dropped into one of the armchairs, and Scout felt compelled and relieved to take the matching one.

"That's interesting, miss," Scout said.

"Isn't it?" She eyed him carefully, and Scout felt self-conscious. He was suddenly thoughtful of his appearance. He ran a damp hand over hair that hadn't been brushed, and when was the last time he'd cleaned his teeth?

"Please call me Carla."

"All right," Scout said, but he couldn't ever imagine calling her anything but Miss Spalding.

Miss Spalding smiled—a smile Scout found vaguely familiar, as if he'd seen Miss Spalding's photograph somewhere—and fluttered her eyelashes, making Scout wonder if she'd got something in her eyes. "When my parents agreed to send me to London to attend Oxford, I just simply couldn't wait to meet you." She tilted her head. "I never dreamed you would be such a handsome young man, though."

Scout stared at his feet. His tongue was tied, and he found it difficult to swallow. And why were his blasted hands sweating so much?

"This sure is a nice house," Miss Spalding said, seemingly appreciating the sitting room decor.

Scout glanced at the swinging door that opened to the dining room and led to the kitchen. Where was Lizzie or Grace with the tea tray?

"So, what do you do for entertainment, Scout?" Miss Spalding asked.

"I play with Boss," Scout said, enthused that she'd asked him an easy question. "That's my dog. Sometimes, my dad takes me to play cricket. I ride horses. That's my favourite thing to do."

Miss Spalding's pretty eyes flashed with interest. "Are the horses on the property?"

"Yes," Scout said, finding his voice. "There's a stable in the back garden. We have two geldings."

"That's fantastic!" Miss Spalding beamed. "We have riding stables in Lowell, and I've become a bit of a horse nut too. I'd love to meet your horses."

Scout found this to be a frightening and yet strangely irresistible prospect.

"It would be my pleasure," he said, using all the etiquette habits he'd been exposed to.

They stood to leave just as Lizzie arrived with the tea.

"Our guest would like to see the back garden," Scout said. "Perhaps you could bring the tea out there?"

"Of course, Master Scout," Lizzie said. She gave the slightest curtsy then turned back through the swinging door.

Scout, feeling rather pleased that Miss Spalding would witness the respect shown to him by their maid, led his guest out of the back entrance, across the garden, and into the stable. He wondered why his legs felt shaky.

24

Ginger rarely felt anything but admiration and respect for Basil, but at this moment, as they raced back to Hartigan House in Basil's Austin, she found her chest was tight with fury.

Vera Sharp was a cunning woman. Her father, Mortimer Sharp, had been imprisoned largely due to Basil's stellar investigative work, and Vera had taken it upon herself to gain revenge.

"How could you not tell me about the threatening note?" Ginger stared straight ahead as she spoke, willing the motorcar to navigate the London streets more quickly.

Constable Braxton and another officer were leading the way in a black police motorcar, sounding the brass horn in a warning to other vehicles, horses and carriages, and pedestrians to make way.

Were she driving, they'd be much further along already!

"I didn't want to worry you," Basil repeated. "You had enough on your mind with baby Rosa."

"But we weren't safe!"

"Ginger, I have a man keeping watch and have had so since I got the note."

Ginger shot Basil a scathing look. "You have a man keeping watch? That loiterer on the court? I've been wary of him for weeks. I've warned Felicia to be careful of him and nearly called the police to report him as a nuisance!"

"I'm sorry—"

"Vera Sharp is a master of disguise, Basil. A formidable nemesis. One man will be nothing for her."

Basil's jaw twitched, and Ginger closed her lips. She had every right to be upset, but her tongue-lashing wasn't helping the situation. She had to believe that Basil had done what he thought was best at the time, and she knew he'd never do anything to endanger their family. She let out a long breath, thankful that Hyde Park was finally in sight.

"Scout was safe at Kingswell," Basil said. "It's

why I thought it was so important to send him there. Mr. Boyle was aware of the situation, but neither of us anticipated that Scout would run away."

"You thought he would be safe at the circus," Ginger said.

"He was with Marvin. I didn't imagine that Vera Sharp had been tailing him and had followed him to the circus, all to get back at me."

"I know," Ginger said. "Forgive me for feeling angry. I'm just frightened for Scout right now." And with good reason. Vera Sharp was without empathy or scruples.

And Ginger was angry with herself. They'd never seen Kiki without face paint. Everyone, including Ginger, had thought it nothing more than an individual quirk. Personal idiosyncrasies amongst circus performers weren't uncommon. But Ginger had seen Vera Sharp up close and was familiar with her ability to disguise herself. How had she missed the signs?

Nearing Mallowan Court, Constable Braxton roared into the cul-de-sac while Basil took the back lane, pulling up beside the garage in the back garden. They hopped out of the motorcar, dashing towards the back door.

Inside, Ginger yelled, "Scout!"

Coming out of the kitchen, Mrs. Beasley, the rotund cook, grabbed at her heart, her doughy face flushed as she gasped with a start. "Mrs. Reed. You frightened me."

"Forgive me," Ginger said. "Have you seen Scout?"

"He was in the kitchen about an hour ago, eating shortbread biscuits and giving your little dog a treat. But I haven't seen him—"

Basil had already darted out of the kitchen, and Ginger left the befuddled cook and followed him down the corridor and across the black-and-white-tiled floor of the entrance hall. Basil whipped open the front door to let the constables inside.

"Braxton, where's Jones?" Basil demanded.

"We found him behind the rose bushes on the ground, sir," Constable Braxton said.

"Dead?" Basil asked with alarm.

"No, sir. He has a mighty bump on his head, but he's alive. Lady Davenport-Witt came upon us as we drove up. She's ringing for a doctor now."

Pippins appeared with a look of concern on his wrinkled face. Standing tall, with hands held behind his back, he asked, "Madam? Might I be of service?"

"Have you seen Scout, Pips?"

"Yes, madam. He had a visitor, an old friend of yours. A Miss Spalding."

Ginger's blood ran cold. She knew of no one named Spalding. Her son was in the hands of a killer.

"Where are they?" she asked.

BASIL CLENCHED his fist as he stared at Lizzie. The maid stood in the hall holding a tray with a teapot, some biscuits, and two cups. As Basil awaited her answer, she stared back, seemingly frozen to the spot, her eyes round and wide open. He asked again, "Have you seen Master Scout?"

Lizzie's knees bent, out of either habit or fear of Basil's stern voice. "The young lady asked to see the horses, sir. They said they'd return shortly for tea."

"Blast it!" Basil said, breaking into a run to the back entrance of the house. He didn't bother telling Ginger to wait. As concerned as he was about what they might find, he knew she'd never obey a direction like that. In fact, despite her heels and cumbersome skirt, she kept up, and was only a few strides behind as they reached the stable doors, swinging them open.

The smell of hay and horse manure met Basil as he adjusted his eyes to the dimmer light inside.

"Scout!"

His Arabian, Sir Blackwell, and Goldmine occupied the first two stalls, but the door of the third stall, which was usually empty, stood wide open. What Basil saw inside stopped him in his tracks. He had known fearful moments in his duties as a policeman, but rarely had he felt such abject terror as he did at this moment. Adrenaline coursed through every vein, and he struggled to maintain control as he slowly raised his palms.

"Vera."

Vera Sharp snarled, her voice chilling Basil to the core. "One more step and I will finish it!"

She was down on one knee, holding a wooden-handled farrier's hoof knife to the neck of the inert form of Scout, who lay face up in the dirt and mud. His eyes were open and slowly blinking as he stared vacantly at the ceiling.

"Sir!" Braxton's voice came from the doorway. Basil motioned for him to stand down, keeping his gaze locked on Vera.

"Vera—"

"I would have got away clean," she said. "It would have worked perfectly if it wasn't for his blasted sweaty hands!" Vera grimaced at Scout. "The little brat kept rubbing it off." She stared back at Basil with a cruel glint in her eye. "I should've known. Like father, like son."

Basil could hardly forget when Vera had used her gloved hands, covered with poison, to grab his face to extinguish his life by poisoning him through his skin.

"I've been watching your little man for a while now, you know," Vera said. "I knew he was at the academy. I saw him leave. Followed him to the circus. How stupendous! Playing the mime was my favourite childhood pastime, and here I had a chance to put my skills to good use. My plan was to blend in and hope that no one would question me too closely. Just another clown recently taken on.

"Scout's outburst promising to kill the ringmaster sparked the idea. I wasn't sure the plan with the elephant would work, of course, but as you saw, it worked splendidly. After all, fortune *does* seem to favour the bold." Vera let out manic laughter, causing the farrier's knife to shake near Scout's neck.

"Just stay calm, Vera," Basil said, trying to keep the desperation out of his voice. "Let's talk about this."

"Oh, yes! Let's talk about it. That'll make it all

better, won't it?" Vera sneered, causing Basil to take in a sharp breath. "No, I want you to remember this. I want you to feel its pain for the rest of your life. You with your fancy home, your high-society wife, your lovely family. You have it all, don't you, Chief Inspector Reed? You don't know what it's like to feel real pain, real loss."

Basil watched in horror as her hand holding the farrier's knife was raised high in the air. Could he get to her in time? His mind raced to calculate the odds.

"Vera . . ."

Her arm started downwards.

"No!"

Then, the sharp crack of a gun firing.

Basil flinched and nearly dropped to the ground. The horses whinnied in alarm.

As if struck with the force of a horse's kick, Vera Sharp was thrown backwards against the wall. The wooden-handled blade dropped out of her hand onto the dirt as blood blossomed on her blouse.

Basil turned to see his wife poised in a perfect shooting stance ten feet behind him. He gulped dryly.

"Ginger?"

25

The palm-sized, silver-handled Remington derringer had been a gift from Ginger's first husband, Daniel. He'd produced the gift box with the small pistol inside the night before leaving her in Boston to return to England to join the King's army to fight in the Great War. It was a token suggesting she would be protected somehow, even if he wasn't around to do it. Growing up in America, she'd been on a shooting range, and when Daniel left, she found firing her new pistol at the range to be therapeutic.

Before long, she'd become a crack shot.

This flashed through Ginger's mind in a split second as a red mark bloomed on Vera Sharp's left shoulder as she slumped to the ground.

"Scout!"

In an instant, Ginger was at Scout's side, grabbing him by the arms and pulling him as far away from Vera as possible.

Basil stared at her with a stunned look then sprang into action, tying Vera's wrist, the one on the uninjured arm, to a post using leather reins that were hanging in the horse stall. To Braxton, he shouted, "Get the doctor!"

Ginger had the vial she'd been carrying in her handbag in her hand. Ever since their last case, after Vera Sharp had escaped the police, Ginger had anticipated a situation such as this. Lucineride had been Vera's poison of choice, and thankfully there was an antidote, though the concoction needed to be ingested as soon as possible after the poisoning.

Lifting Scout's head, she said, "Love, you have to drink this."

He groaned as she pressed the rim of the vial to his lips, and she was worried she was too late, that he wouldn't be able to swallow. Boss whined, pawing Scout's arm in encouragement.

"Come now, Scout," Ginger said with urgency. "You can do this. Just one swallow." As Ginger pushed the vial deeper into his mouth, she stroked his throat downward, hoping to trigger a swallowing reflex. She held her breath. If Scout choked it up instead of swallowing, he would be lost. She only had one vial.

Then Scout gulped, and the antidote was delivered.

Oh mercy, such blessed relief!

Now all Ginger could do was hold her son and wait. It'd been a long time since she'd truly held on to him—too long. His body had changed, even in the few weeks he'd been attending boarding school. His arms and back were sinewy with more defined muscles. Gone was the skinny, spindly child with a gap-tooth smile and new teeth too large for his face. Ginger stroked the forehead of this new young-man version of her son, his features promising a handsome fellow about to emerge.

"You two are going to bring me to tears."

Vera had lost consciousness at first, and there was a moment when Ginger had wondered if she was dead, though she'd quite deliberately shot her in a manner that wouldn't mean automatic death. Basil, on one knee, held a handkerchief to Vera's wound, staying the bleeding, but Vera seemed unaware of his presence behind her.

Vera's breathing hitched as she continued. "My ma never loved me." After a breath, "Not like that. I was a burden." Another gulp of air was followed by, "The men didn't like her anymore when they learned she had a young'un." She turned her head and held Ginger's gaze. "Then, as I got older, the men wanted me, and she hated me for it."

She continued with her laboured breath. "Pa had a way of making me feel special. Wanted. I spent every waking moment waiting for him to come back to me, and when he did, I felt like I could walk on clouds. He would've come for me if your husband hadn't put him in prison."

Ginger felt a wave of pity for the woman. The man she so admired, the one she was willing to kill for, had been the first to abandon her. Vera's childlike mind didn't see it that way, though. She'd missed the part where Mortimer Sharp had left her, viewing him as a pseudo-saviour.

"I'm sorry," Ginger said. "Life hasn't been fair for you."

"Don't!" Vera shouted. "Don't you pity me!"

"I don't pity you," Ginger said. "I'm showing empathy. You should try it sometime."

Basil cut in with a nod towards Scout. "How is he?"

Scout stirred in Ginger's arms. "I'm fine, Dad," he whispered. "I'll be all right."

Once the ambulance arrived, Vera was taken to the hospital accompanied by Constable Braxton. Scout had gained back enough energy that Ginger and Basil could assist him to his room, the doctor following behind. Boss skipped along in front with a sense of purpose, refusing to leave Scout's side.

Standing by his bedroom door, Ginger watched Scout fall asleep safely tucked in his bed. In that moment she vowed to do whatever was necessary to ensure her son would be safe, that her whole family would be safe, no matter what it took. She'd take them all back to Boston, if need be.

26

The early morning air felt crisp and clean to Scout as he and his father came to a stop atop a small ridge in Kensington Gardens north of Hartigan House. Seeing his breath in the air reminded Scout of his climb up the small hill south of Clapham Common to view the circus below. So much had changed since then, and he himself most of all. Like the miracle of the change of seasons, winter into spring, a cold heart had turned to warm.

He and his dad were astride Goldmine and Sir Blackwell, his dad letting him ride the Akhal-Teke at Scout's own request. It had taken him a while to master the art of riding, something he loved to do more than anything.

Today, it made him think of Tulip. The circus

had moved on from London, north towards Scotland. Scout's only regret was that he hadn't had a chance to say goodbye to his large friend. Elephants had long life spans, so Scout took comfort in the notion that perhaps he would see her again someday.

The late-spring air caused a mist to rise from the Serpentine, creating a mystical scene as a pair of sophisticated white swans swam by.

The morning sun was gaining strength, and father and son sat with their eyes closed and faces turned towards it. To Scout, it felt luxurious, like a moment to be savoured.

"You seem unusually quiet this morning," his father said after a moment.

"Do I?" Scout blinked, keeping his gaze straight ahead.

"You've hardly said a word since we left the stable. Not something I'm used to from you."

His father considered him with a small, curious smile.

"I suppose I'm in a thoughtful mood this morning."

"Nothing wrong with being thoughtful." His dad scratched his chin under the strap of his riding helmet. "In fact, for a young man like yourself, perhaps it's a good sign. It means you're well on your way to that thing in life called 'growing up'."

His father's compliment made Scout feel curiously warm in his chest. Few men in his life had given him the proper kind of praise. A pat on the back for nicking a loaf of bread or picking a pocket of its contents and not getting caught didn't count. Whenever he heard it from his father, it reached in and touched something deep inside of him in a way he didn't understand. His mother's praise always made him feel like he was worth something—like he belonged. His father's praise made him feel stronger, more like the man he hoped to become.

"I want to be the best son to you and Mum and the best brother to Rosa." Scout was surprised at the words as they were almost unbidden from his lips. But even as he said them, he knew they were the most powerful words he had ever uttered.

"I believe you do have it in you," his father said, staring him in the eye. "And if you remember those words, your life will be one of satisfaction, and it will be filled with the kind of riches that don't come from material wealth."

"Yes, sir." Scout breathed, feeling a little embarrassed by the verbal intimacy. "I only wish Marvin could understand just a little."

"Marvin has his own road to walk," his father said. "Hopefully, his journey will grow smoother over time."

They headed out of the park, reaching the lane that led to the back garden of Hartigan House.

"Speaking of those kinds of riches," his dad said brightly, pointing down towards the rear of the house, "I believe your mother and your sister mean to meet us."

Scout thought his mother, with her bright red hair and deep green eyes, was the most beautiful lady in the world. Her smile was so radiant that it rivalled the sun that morning. Baby Rosa, with her full cheeks and tiny mouth, was asleep in their mother's arms.

And to think he'd almost thrown all of it into the rubbish. It made his stomach turn with shame.

"Breakfast is ready, you two," Mum said as they rode closer. "I hope you're both hungry."

"Famished," said Dad, dismounting. Scout did the same, and they handed the reins of both geldings to Clement, who was standing at the ready.

Thanking the groundskeeper, Scout and his father followed Ginger inside. Ginger paused to smile at him, and he returned the gesture, thankful that he'd finally grown into his big teeth. He placed his fingers on his little sister's cheek, taking in the sweetness of the promise represented, and impulsively kissed the baby on her head.

He whispered in her ear, "Big brother will always be here for you, little Rosa. I promise."

GINGER THREW herself back into the routine of baby care and work. At present, she was in her study at Hartigan House, running through orders for fabrics and factory dresses for Feathers & Flair, and writing cheques to pay outstanding invoices. Though she enjoyed the hustle and bustle of the shop, when she needed to focus on numbers, the sanctuary of her study suited her better.

However, it wasn't enough busy work to keep her mind completely off the murders at the circus. Her pulse still raced when she thought of how close they'd come to losing Scout, how close they had been to a darker, more tragic outcome. The worst was when the "what ifs" flooded her mind and cooled her blood. *What if Scout's pubescent body hadn't responded with sweaty palms at the sight of a pretty girl and the poison had penetrated more thoroughly? What if she and Basil had arrived at the stables a minute later and Vera had used that knife on Scout's neck? What if she'd missed her shot with the Remington?* She hadn't had a lot of shooting practice lately, and her skills might've lessened.

Ginger closed her eyes as she inhaled deeply, then slowly exhaled. She had to stop her mind from going to what might've been and hold on tight to what was. The poison hadn't worked, Vera hadn't succeeded with the knife, and her own shooting skills had been up to par.

"He's still with us, Bossy," she said aloud. Her pet, curled up as he liked to do in his bed near the fireplace still warm with glowing coal, raised his cute little black-and-white head at the sound of his name. "That's what we have to focus on. He's here, and we can be happy."

Luther Bancroft and Prince Natukunda didn't have this option, their lives taken from them most cruelly. The murder of Mr. Bancroft was one of opportunity and a shot in the dark that Vera could use to implicate Scout. It was a chess move with a risk that had gone her way. Poor Prince Natukunda, known also as Billy Smith, had become a liability. Vera had confessed that he had indeed deduced that her mime act was a façade, and that "Kiki" wasn't a male. She'd scoffed at the pittance he'd requested as part of his blackmail scheme, as if any price could enslave her.

At first glance, Vera Sharp looked as harmless and unassuming as any woman one would pass by in the streets, but her heart was black and her mind unsound. As Ginger had predicted, a plea of insanity had been entered by her solicitor on her account, and it was likely she'd escape the noose and would spend the rest of her days at the Broadmoor asylum, the prison for the criminally insane. Ginger imagined they'd have to be extremely diligent, as one who was as much a master of disguise and with as unscrupulous cunning as Vera Sharp could never be underestimated.

The most important thing was that they still had Scout. Benefitting from his healthy body, the antidote had worked. He'd also had a change of heart and mind, the experience catapulting him out of childhood. No longer a sulky, spiteful lad, he'd declared that he wanted to make the most of his life and his new privileges—a gift he no longer took for granted. Ginger wondered, as the teen years progressed, how many times she'd have to remind him of his bold statement.

Ginger was pulled from her reverie by the unscheduled arrival of Felicia.

"I hope I'm not interrupting," Felicia said, stepping inside. "I'm just popping in to say hello."

"Always a pleasure. What brings you here?"

"I've returned with Grandmama—she insisted I accompany her to Mrs. Schofield's to play Whist. Grandmama is convinced that your neighbour cheats at cards. But I didn't see evidence of it, a fact that has Grandmama's feathers ruffled."

"Those two have a reluctant attraction," Ginger said.

"I do have some good news." Felicia stepped in further and took one of the empty leather chairs. "I broke down and told Charles my troubles with Burton. I failed at keeping my distress to myself. Apparently, I wear my emotions on my sleeve!"

Ginger chuckled. "That's not such a bad thing, love."

"Well, I cried on Charles' shoulder, which is rather embarrassing. I blubbered on about how I'm used to the staff being like family. I admit I was overcome with sentiment about Mrs. Beasley, Clement, Lizzie, and Pippins. Especially Pippins. I'm fond of them, and I feel like a failure that I'm not liked in my own home."

"Oh, Felicia." Ginger wished her desk wasn't separating her from her former sister-in-law but resisted making a scene by going to her to embrace her.

"It turned out for the best," Felicia continued. "Charles talked to Burton, giving him an ultimatum, and Burton's been on his best behaviour ever since."

"That's fantastic!"

"It is, isn't it?" Felicia's expression stiffened as her lips grew tight. She blinked as her eyes grew teary. Clearly, her sleeves weren't the only place she could wear her emotions.

"Felicia?"

"Oh, Ginger!" Felicia raised her gloved hands to her face as she cried.

"What is it?" Ginger said. "I thought things were good?"

"They are," Felicia said, retrieving a handkerchief from her handbag. "I'm being silly. I don't know what's the matter with me these days. I'm crying at the drop of a hat."

Ginger pulled back to look steadily at Felicia. "Has anything else changed recently? Perhaps more frequent trips to the loo? Tenderness in the bosom?"

Felicia stared back, her jaw growing slack. "Yes. I thought I'd had flu."

"You might need to visit your physician, Felicia."

A smile pulled across Ginger's lips. "You could be in the family way."

"Oh no, you don't think—"

Ginger laughed. "It's the natural way of things."

"Oh, I'm speechless." Felicia did look rather pale suddenly. "I can hardly think."

"Perhaps a little tea?"

Felicia shook her head. "No, I've had my fill at Mrs. Scofield's, and just the mention of tea makes me want to run to the loo!"

Felicia's good news filled Ginger's thoughts, and she chuckled at how Felicia practically ran from her office, determined to use the facilities in her own house. It was hard to focus on the correspondence that remained on her desk. Pippins arrived with the post, and Ginger counted her blessings as she welcomed him in, so grateful to have the staff she cared deeply for and that those sentiments were returned.

He offered a silver tray that held a small pile of white envelopes. "And I thought that I'd nearly finished," Ginger said, smiling.

"In my life, madam, I've found that one's list is never completed," Pippins said, his cornflower-blue eyes twinkling. "It simply gets added to again and again."

Ginger chuckled. "How true!" She gazed at her butler with fondness. He'd been in service all of his life, and a good part of it with her family. Ginger realised she didn't really know that much about him. It wasn't due to her lack of interest, but societal propriety didn't allow for shared intimacies between the classes. It was unseemly to pry. One just never asked.

Perhaps one day, she'd toss propriety out of the window. It wasn't like Pippins would be with them forever. The thought of a world without him made her gasp, and she was suddenly overcome with anticipatory grief.

"Are you all right, madam?" Pippins asked with sincere concern.

Ginger quickly pulled herself together. "Yes, of course. Thank you for the post."

Pippins bowed and backed out of the room. "Madam."

Flipping through the envelopes, Ginger tossed each one onto her desk to attend to later.

The last one, simply addressed to Mr. and Mrs. Reed with cursive leaning to the left, made her heart stop.

It couldn't be from Vera! She was in custody, and they'd never permit her to write to them.

Ripping the envelope open, Ginger pulled the notepaper out, the words jumping, swimming as if they'd escaped the page.

Well played.
And guess what? I have a parole date.
Your friend, Mortimer Sharp.

Ginger slumped in her chair as she stared at the similar familial handwriting.

Oh mercy.

Not again.

———

Don't miss the next Ginger Gold mystery~
MURDER AT THE BOXING CLUB

Murder's a knockout!

Despite her misgivings and general distaste for fighting sports, Mrs. Ginger Reed, also known as Lady Gold, agrees to attend a boxing match to support the cousin of her adopted son, a street fighter who's quickly risen in the ranks.

But when his opponent, the presumed champion-to-be, drops out and then drops dead, Ginger and her husband, Basil, a chief inspector at Scotland Yard, investigate. Was the fighter dead because of sports-betting gone awry? Were London gangs involved? And has an old, but newly present danger returned to threaten the Reed family?

When one of their own falls prey, the gloves come off and the fight becomes personal. Can Ginger and Basil save their family and stop a killer before the towel is thrown in the ring?

Buy on AMAZON or read Free with Kindle Unlimited!

———

ABOUT LUCINERIDE

Invented "science" is a common ploy in all kinds of fictitious works including books, film and television.

In Murder at the Circus the drug *Lucineride* is a creation of the author's imagination.

GINGER GOLD'S JOURNAL

Sign up for Lee's readers list and gain access to **Ginger Gold's private Journal.** Find out about Ginger's Life before the SS *Rosa* and how she became the woman she has. This is a fluid document that will cover her romance with her late husband Daniel, her time serving in the British secret service during World War One, and beyond. Includes a recipe for Dark Dutch Chocolate Cake!

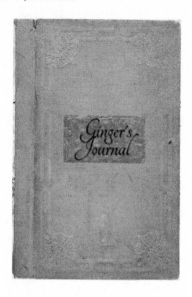

It begins:**July 31, 1912**

How fabulous that I found this Journal today, hidden in the bottom of my wardrobe. Good old Pippins, our English butler in London, gave it to me as a parting gift when Father whisked me away on our American adventure so he could marry Sally. Pips said it was for me to record my new adventures. I'm ashamed I never even penned one word before today. I think I was just too sad.

This old leather-bound journal takes me back to that emotional time. I had shed enough tears to fill the ocean and I remember telling

Father dramatically that I was certain to cause flooding to match God's. At eight years old I was well-trained in my biblical studies, though, in retro-spect, I would say that I had probably bordered on heresy with my little tantrum.

The first week of my "adventure" was spent with a tummy ache and a number of embarrassing sessions that involved a bucket and Father holding back my long hair so I wouldn't soil it with vomit.

I certainly felt that I was being punished for some reason. Hartigan House—though large and sometimes lonely—was my home and Pips was my good friend. He often helped me to pass the time with games of I Spy and Xs and Os.

"Very good, Little Miss," he'd say with a twinkle in his blue eyes when I won, which I did often. I suspect now that our good butler wasn't beyond letting me win even when unmerited.

Father had got it into his silly head that I needed a mother, but I think the truth was he wanted a wife. Sally, a woman half my father's age, turned out to be a sufficient wife in the end, but I could never claim her as a mother.

Well, Pips, I'm sure you'd be happy to know that things turned out all right here in America.

SUBSCRIBE to read more!

.

ACKNOWLEDGMENTS

A big shout out to my husband, Norm Strauss, who joined writing forces with me a while ago to help with the Lady Gold Investigations short story series and the Rosa Reed Mystery series.

Until now, I've penned all of the Ginger Gold Mystery series novels on my own, but Norm has recently joined me as a ghost writer. Two heads are better than one!

ABOUT THE AUTHOR

Lee Strauss is a USA TODAY bestselling author of The Ginger Gold Mysteries series, The Higgins & Hawke Mystery series, The Rosa Reed Mystery series (cozy historical mysteries), A Nursery Rhyme Mystery series (mystery suspense), The Light & Love series (sweet romance), The Clockwise Collection (YA time travel romance), and young adult historical fiction with over a million books read. She has titles published in German and French, and a growing audio library.

When Lee's not writing or reading she likes to cycle, hike, and stare at the ocean. She loves to drink caffè lattes and red wines in exotic places, and eat dark chocolate anywhere.

For more info on books by Lee Strauss and her social media links, visit leestraussbooks.com. To make sure you don't miss the next new release, be sure to sign up for her readers' list!

Discuss the books, ask questions, share your

opinions. Fun giveaways! Join the Lee Strauss Readers' Group on Facebook for more info.

Did you know you can follow your favourite authors on Bookbub? If you subscribe to Bookbub — (and if you don't, why don't you? - They'll send you daily emails alerting you to sales and new releases on just the kind of books you like to read!) — follow me to make sure you don't miss the next Ginger Gold Mystery!

www.leestraussbooks.com

leestraussbooks@gmail.com

MORE FROM LEE STRAUSS

On AMAZON

GINGER GOLD MYSTERY SERIES (cozy 1920s historical)

Cozy. Charming. Filled with Bright Young Things. This Jazz Age murder mystery will entertain and delight you with its 1920s flair and pizzazz!

Murder on the SS Rosa

Murder at Hartigan House

Murder at Bray Manor

Murder at Feathers & Flair

Murder at the Mortuary

Murder at Kensington Gardens

Murder at St. George's Church

The Wedding of Ginger & Basil

Murder Aboard the Flying Scotsman

Murder at the Boat Club

Murder on Eaton Square

Murder by Plum Pudding

Murder on Fleet Street

Murder at Brighton Beach

Murder in Hyde Park

Murder at the Royal Albert Hall

Murder in Belgravia

Murder on Mallowan Court

Murder at the Savoy

Murder at the Circus

Murder in France

LADY GOLD INVESTIGATES (Ginger Gold companion short stories)

Volume 1

Volume 2

Volume 3

Volume 4

HIGGINS & HAWKE MYSTERY SERIES (cozy 1930s historical)

The 1930s meets Rizzoli & Isles in this friendship depression era cozy mystery series.

Death at the Tavern

Death on the Tower

Death on Hanover

Death by Dancing

THE ROSA REED MYSTERIES

(1950s cozy historical)

Murder at High Tide

Murder on the Boardwalk

Murder at the Bomb Shelter

Murder on Location

Murder and Rock 'n Roll

Murder at the Races

Murder at the Dude Ranch

Murder in London

Murder at the Fiesta

Murder at the Weddings

**A NURSERY RHYME MYSTERY
SERIES(mystery/sci fi)**

*Marlow finds himself teamed up with intelligent and savvy
Sage Farrell, a girl so far out of his league he feels blinded in
her presence - literally - damned glasses! Together they work*

to find the identity of *@gingerbreadman. Can they stop the
killer before he strikes again?*

Gingerbread Man

Life Is but a Dream

Hickory Dickory Dock

Twinkle Little Star

LIGHT & LOVE (sweet romance)

*Set in the dazzling charm of Europe, follow Katja, Gabriella,
Eva, Anna and Belle as they find strength, hope and love.*

Love Song

Your Love is Sweet

In Light of Us

Lying in Starlight

PLAYING WITH MATCHES (WW2 history/romance)

*A sobering but hopeful journey about how one young
German boy copes with the war and propaganda. Based on
true events.*

A Piece of Blue String (companion short story)

THE CLOCKWISE COLLECTION (YA time travel romance)

Casey Donovan has issues: hair, height and uncontrollable trips to the 19th century! And now this ~ she's accidentally taken Nate Mackenzie, the cutest boy in the school, back in time. Awkward.

Clockwise

Clockwiser

Like Clockwork

Counter Clockwise

Clockwork Crazy

Clocked (companion novella)

Standalones

Seaweed

Love, Tink

Made in the USA
Las Vegas, NV
27 August 2022

54124128R00146